FLAME IN FIJI

Robyn ... ...
years of her brother Johnny, so she was doubly
excited when he invited her to go and help him
run his guesthouse – in Fiji! But she arrived in
the Pacific to discover that it wasn't only
Johnny who was running the guesthouse.
There was that disturbing David Kinnear as
well . . .

FLAME IN FIJI

BY

GLORIA BEVAN

MILLS & BOON LIMITED
17-19 FOLEY STREET
LONDON W1A 1DR

First published 1973
This edition 1973

© Gloria Bevan 1973

ISBN 0 263 71501 9

*Made and Printed in Great Britain by
C. Nicholls & Company Ltd
The Philips Park Press, Manchester*

To
Mrs. Brenda McDougall
with happy memories of Fleet Street
last August

CHAPTER 1

LAST night when Robyn had stepped from the plane into the warm perfumed air of Nandi International Airport it was long past midnight. She had been met by a smiling Fijian taxi-driver in his kilt-like peaked sulu and immediately whirled away through the darkness and up a flare-lighted path leading to the luxuriously appointed Travelodge Hotel. In her suite she had slipped into bed without even bothering to draw the curtains. Now in the freshness of early morning she was aware of a delicious sense of warmth. Lying back against the pillows, arms crossed behind her head and long dark-blonde hair streaming around her shoulders, she stared bemusedly out at her unfamiliar surroundings.

Softly waving coconut palms with their clusters of fruit brushed the wide picture windows and beyond swept the lush green of sugar-cane plantations. Along a path cut between the patchwork of greens strolled big-framed, dark-skinned women with an erect carriage and graceful walk. Their long vividly-patterned cotton frocks swirled around bare brown ankles and umbrellas shielded curly black heads from the already hot Fijian sun. Behind them straggled neatly-dressed children, school satchels slung over small shoulders. Over the harbour of Lautoka jagged mountain peaks were wreathed in drifting cloud. It was all incredibly fresh and colourful, a delight.

I'm really here in Fiji – at last! The thought made her leap from bed and soon she was taking a warm shower, slipping into a cool short shift and pushing her feet into the thonged sandals that had been put away since last summer back home in New Zealand. Home ... maybe this was to be her home from now on, these scattered islands in the South Pacific. A light touch of lipstick, eye make-up, and she was ready to face the day. She moved along the wide carpeted corridor, passing happy young Fijian housegirls with their un-hurried manner and welcoming smile. Outside she was met by a dazzle of sunlight. It sequined the waters of the great blue pool, glistened on the flaring petals of the enormously large hibiscus blossoms that edged the pool and splashed vividly green lawns on either side of the pathway with patches of crimson, bronze, pink, yellow.

"Wouldn't you just know," a friendly feminine voice with an American accent spoke at her side, "that you were in Fiji, just by the scent of the frangipani?"

"Wouldn't you!" Robyn smiled towards the faultlessly groomed middle-aged woman who passed her on the covered walkway. She glanced towards the bushes dotting the lawns where satiny frangipani flowers in pink and cream perfumed the warm clear air.

Still agreeably conscious of an unaccustomed sense of well-being in the warm sunshine, Robyn strolled along the wind-ing path between the cool covering of thatched coconut palm, pausing for a few moments to glance in at the small gift shop with its display of shell jewellery and coloured coral, brightly printed loose frocks, gay woven baskets and sunhats. Then she moved into the restaurant already crowded with tourists pausing for a short stay at this crossroads of the Pacific. Robyn supposed that many of the guests already seated there were like herself breakfasting early in order to be in time to catch the daily bus leaving for the Coral Coast. Or perhaps they planned to go on one of the various sea excursions to the out-lying islands leaving daily from the wharf at Lautoka.

In the softly shaded room with its tapa-cloth hung walls and glowing carved lamps made from native timbers, a young Indian waiter led her towards a corner table. "I'm sorry," he murmured apologetically, "but there are no vacant tables this morning. If madam wouldn't mind sharing –"

"Of course not. This will be fine, thank you." She glanced towards the man already seated there, a dark burly young man whose brief upward glance appraised with interest the tall girl with clear grey eyes and wide lips upturned at the

8

corners. Robyn noticed that in common with most of the other men in the room he wore an open-necked shirt printed in a design of primitive art, and his smile, she couldn't help thinking, was really something.

She seated herself opposite to him and brown eyes in a tanned face twinkled towards her. "*Bula!*"

She stared across at him bewilderedly, then remembered that *bula* was the word with which the smiling young Fijian maids had greeted her a few moments previously.

"I can see," he was saying pleasantly, "that you're a new arrival in the islands –"

She laughed, unfolding her napkin. Somehow it was easy to laugh with this relaxed and pleasant stranger in these enchanting tropical surroundings. "That's right. By the midnight plane from New Zealand. I take it that '*bula*' is the local word for 'good morning'?"

He nodded. "Or good night, or good day, how are you, hello. You'll hear it all around the place. It seems that Bula is one of the ancient Fijian deities. There he is, up there on the wall, looking down on you! By rights you're supposed to bow to him and acknowledge his presence!"

Dark blonde hair swept her shoulders as her curious gaze went towards the carved mask on the wall above. Garlanded with beads and shells, the narrow pointed face stared down at her from inscrutable sightless eyes. "He looks ... formidable. But it's a good carving."

He nodded. "You'll come across lots of these masks around Fiji. The natives carve them out of the timber of the rain-tree." His eyes on the menu outspread in well-shaped hands, he added pleasantly, "Staying long in the islands?"

She hesitated. "That depends." All at once the soft warm atmosphere, the novelty and excitement of her surroundings took over and the words spilled eagerly from her lips. "Back in New Zealand where I come from, I've been looking forward to this holiday for years –"

His quizzical glance swept the sensitive young face.

"Years?"

9

"Yes, honestly!" Illogically she found herself thinking that he had an infectious smile. Maybe it was the warmth in his eyes that made his smile so heartwarming. "You see, I happen to have a share in some property here."

"Lucky you!"

"But do you know, I've never ever seen it!" Her face was alight with the eagerness and enthusiasm of youth. "So many things kept happening to stop me from making the trip! First of all I was too young –"

"Too *young*?" Now he appeared to be genuinely taken aback.

"Uh-huh, I told you." Clear grey eyes swept up to meet his attentive gaze. "It's been years. I guess the main reason why I never came before was because somehow or other I always managed to spend the fare money I'd saved up."

"But you finally made it?"

"And am I glad I did!"

At that moment a young Fijian waitress, a pink hibiscus blossom tucked in short-cropped curly black hair, paused at their table. Robyn noticed that her companion selected the same light fare she had chosen for her own breakfast – pineapple juice, sliced papaya, toast, black coffee.

As he gave the order she stole a glance towards him and approved of what she saw. Not over tall or wildly good-looking and yet . . . She couldn't think what it was about him that attracted her so, gave her this absurd feeling that she had known him for ages. She only knew she felt happy and relaxed with him and yet at the same time, in some odd way she couldn't explain, strangely excited.

"And you," she asked lightly, "what brings you out to this part of the world? Apart from chasing the sun, I mean?" For she surmised from his cultured accents that he came from England.

"Oh, I'm no tourist, though I have to admit that I did start off that way. That was the idea originally. Blame it on a particularly persuasive poster in a travel agency that chanced to catch my eye one morning when I was on my way

10

to the London office. "Come to Fiji," it said. "Visit the isles of endless summer." He smiled companionably. "Actually I had ideas before that of getting away from it all. I'd been working fairly steadily for a few years without a break, and besides," for a moment the smiling face sobered, "there was something else, a personal reason, why I wanted a change of scene."

Away from what? Robyn wondered. A love affair that had gone wrong? A woman he had loved? She brought her mind back to the deep, vibrant tones.

"So I thought I'd give myself a break between jobs. Architecture is what I happen to be interested in and I'd never been out to this part of the world. A short holiday in the sun, that's all I had in mind when I left London. That was two years ago. What kept me here first was that I got a chance of drawing up the plans for one of the big new tourist hotels that are springing up along the Coral Coast. It was a big job – meant bulldozing an area for putting in a swimming pool, making a causeway to the lagoon, landscaping the grounds with a terraced garden and tropical plants. It took a lot longer than I'd reckoned on for the builders to get to the finishing line. But at that time I had no idea of the way of life out here in the South Pacific. I wasn't taking into account factors like the humid heat, island labour and that carefree feeling that affects everyone out here, whether you realise it or not. You have to put up a real fight against it if you want to get anything done!"

"I suppose so." She reflected that for all his easy manner she couldn't imagine this man allowing anything to get the better of him, not even the enervating climate or the lazy island atmosphere. She brought her mind back to what he was saying.

"There've been no end of hold-ups all along the line. Staffing problems, endless delays waiting for building materials to arrive by ship from overseas, transport difficulties on the islands – but now we've just about got to the end of it. I had a hand in the interior design side of it too, something I took

11

up as a hobby in the first place and it sort of grew. That's why I've just been over to Sydney for a few days. I wanted to get a line on what was available over there in the way of the latest in drapes, furnishings, lighting, for a first-class hotel out here. There was some terrific stuff in the warehouses. I've put the orders in, so now I'm hoping they won't be too long in getting the stuff shipped over here. After that I've got something else lined up – a different set-up altogether this time, the modernising of an old place into a modern tourist apartment block and restaurant. It will be the first place of this type I've worked on in a tropical climate, but it won't be the only one to be updated along the Coral Coast. Out here in Fiji things are going right ahead in the tourist line! It's one of the few unspoilt places left in the world, somewhere where life goes on much as it did centuries ago – and suddenly tourism is becoming big business! There's a constant stream of air travellers arriving here from the States, Canada, England – all over the world!" He took a sip of pineapple juice. "There was a time not so long ago when as far as tourist accommodation went on these islands, you could get away with any old lodging house, ancient fans for cooling, indifferent cuisine. Now, wham! Overnight the whole picture's changing. Inconvenient, old-time hotels and apartment houses have to be updated, or go out of business. Not that I'm complaining about staying on in Fiji. The climate suits me fine and the problems sort themselves out in the end. One thing that makes it all worthwhile is that the end result is pretty satisfying. You see something you've dreamed up eventually take shape, come to life ... something lasting. You know what I mean?"

"I can imagine." Robyn was facing the disturbing conclusion his words had forced on her. When she considered the luxuriously modern hotel in which she was seated at this moment, equal to anything of its type overseas ... With such a standard of accommodation from which to make a choice, who would prefer to spend precious holiday time in an outdated old guesthouse with scarcely any modern amenities,

12

even if it offered a cheaper tariff? She jerked her mind back to the enthusiastic tones.

"The way I see it, today's air travellers expect top accommodation, air-conditioning, modern decor, swimming pools, professional chefs in the kitchen . . . and they're willing to pay for it. So far as I'm concerned, I'm going to see that they get what they want –" He broke off, his swift perceptive glance taking in the long dark lashes shielding Robyn's downcast eyes, the sensitive face from which all the eager excitement had fled. "Sorry, I guess I'm boring you. Once I get up on my hobbyhorse I get carried away. You should have stopped me."

"No, no," she smiled the wide friendly smile that lighted the gravity of her face. "I can see," she said, choosing the words carefully, "what marvellous opportunities there must be here for you, for anyone in the building or tourist trades. All the new modern hotels and apartments. It must be very . . . interesting."

"That's not the word for it! It's darn stimulating. Out here where life goes on just as it did centuries ago, you can get a chance to come to terms with natural surroundings. And with everything connected with tourism going ahead like wildfire I can really get my teeth into the decorating side of things. There's tremendous scope here for anyone with a shred of imagination. Take the native culture, it's got endless possibilities – carving, weaving, ceramics, tapa-cloth, primitive designs and cave drawings. Fantastic materials to work with! To me it's a whole new world to play with. The name's David, by the way, David Kinnear."

She smiled across at him. Something about this man, maybe it was his enthusiastic approach to his work, drew her, gave her a funny glad feeling that he too was staying on here. She hadn't minded travelling alone. After all, it was only a few hours' flying time from the misty north New Zealand winter to the hot sunshine of Fiji. Nevertheless it was comforting to know someone else besides her brother. Come to that, it was quite possible that he wasn't here at all, but away

13

on his schooner somewhere amongst the three hundred odd islands of the Fiji group.

Back in her spacious suite she stuffed her pyjamas inside her overnight travel bag, added a hairbrush, big curlers and make-up kit. Then she paused, struck by a sudden tempting thought. Johnny wasn't expecting her, chances were he wouldn't even be at the Islander to welcome her to the guest-house on the Coral Coast, so why not take full advantage of this sparkling day and go on one of the sea excursions running to one of the outlying islands? "A trip out to one of the islands is the highlight of a visit to Fiji," Johnny had told her, and seeing that today she had a perfect opportunity ... Crossing the room, she leafed through a pile of excursion brochures lying on the bedside table. Apparently there was a variety of outings from which to choose, but she was fascinated by a picture of a fully rigged sailing schooner, the *Seaspray*, due to leave in an hour's time for a day of swimming and beachcombing, sunbathing and shell-collecting, at Castaway Island. All at once her mind was made up and moving towards her suitcase she snapped the catches and bent to take out a floral beach towel, a gay pink swimsuit. As the label caught her eye a smile twitched the corners of her lips. Robyn Carlisle, passenger American Airlines to Fiji. Tomorrow she would reach her destination on the Coral Coast. End of a journey. End of a dream. Lovely thought that before long she and her brother would be together again, after all these years!

She could barely remember a time when she had been part of a family, a real family of her own, for she and Johnny had been young children when their parents had parted for the last time. Robyn retained a vague impression of a mother who was gay and restless, of a father who, even in a child's eyes, appeared so much older than his wife. Maybe their mother hadn't wanted either her or Johnny to come along and complicate her life. How could she ever have cared for them? For immediately their father had left his wife and family, the two children found themselves boarded out with kindly

14

neighbours, then later, with not-so-kindly strangers, while all the time their mother pursued her own interests in the fashion world. As a buyer employed by a leading city store with branches throughout the country, her work took her far away and eventually overseas. For a year or two the two children received at long intervals coloured postcards from various parts of Australia, then later from the United States. After that there was only the silence, and a fading memory of a mother they had scarcely known.

As to their father, beyond a vague knowledge that he had gone to live "somewhere in the Islands" she and Johnny heard nothing from him through the years. Remembering his endless preoccupation with paints and sketchbooks Robyn sometimes wondered, when she thought of him at all, if perhaps he had gone to further his hobby of painting in the clear air and intensity of colour that had for so long drawn artists to the scattered islands of the Pacific. But whatever the reason for his island existence, he never took the trouble to acquaint either her or Johnny with his whereabouts. The single reminder they had of him was the regular six-monthly remittance that reached them from Suva. Forwarded through a lawyer's office in Fiji, the cheques were immediately swallowed up in payment of boarding school fees.

To Robyn school years were a dreary succession of holidays spent with relatives where she felt she wasn't really welcome. It would have been more bearable if only she and Johnny could have been together during the term breaks, but he was four years her senior and they had been separated from the time of the break-up of their parents' marriage.

Then out of the blue had come a letter from Fiji. Robyn had read the dry legal phrasing through twice before fully taking in the meaning of it all. For it informed her of the death of her father, Andrew Carlisle, and went on to state that under the terms of the will she and her brother John were now joint owners of a guesthouse situated on the Coral Coast of Fiji in the Pacific group. There was in addition a small legacy for them both.

Johnny received the news the same week. He wrote her from a small coastal town in the north where he was employed as one of the crew of a fishing vessel. "I'm going out there right away to see what the place is like. If it's okay I may stay and manage it. Why don't you get a school friend to come with you and take a trip out to Fiji in the holidays? Don't forget the place is half yours!"

That was four years ago and in all that time she hadn't made the journey out to the islands to see her brother. She had been content to leave the management of the property in his hands, at least until she reached the age of twenty-one. Occasionally, and always at Christmas time, she received word from him. Once he enclosed in his letter a colour snap depicting a hot blue sea, white sand, tossing coconut palms. But he wasn't a good correspondent. His scribbled notes gave little information about the guesthouse he now managed and she gathered that his interest was all with the sea. The letters were filled with accounts of deep-sea fishing, of giant tortoises, of trading schooners voyaging around the scattered islands, meetings with yachtsmen whose ocean-going craft had brought them half way across the world to the warm reef-enclosed waters of the South Pacific.

As for herself, she had inherited her father's sketching ability and it had never occurred to her to earn her living in any other way than in some form of art work. Fortunately a scholarship awarded her on leaving college had given her a course at art school and the dwindling profits from a half-share in a far-away guesthouse on a South Pacific coast had met expenses for living costs plus the few extras she allowed herself on a spartan budget. Shortly after gaining her Diploma of Fine Arts she began work in the studio of the city's most progressive store. She enjoyed fashion drawing and might have been content to stay indefinitely, had not Johnny come strolling into the store to see her on one bleak winter day. Johnny! So strong and bronzed, his thatch of light hair bleached straw-colour by the hot Fijian sunlight, the rakish grin she remembered so well.

16

Had it not been for the undeniable likeness between them no one in the studio would have believed her when she had told them she was going out to lunch with her brother! Oh, it was wonderful to see him again! That was one of the disadvantages of a lonely, unwanted childhood. It did things to you, made you cling to the few relatives you possessed, be over-anxious to trust anyone you liked, like the boy-friends with whom she had imagined herself to be wildly in love. Until with a painful shock had come the realisation that actually she was enamoured of an idealistic picture built up in her own mind. Not like Johnny. She'd never be disappointed in him. He would never let her down.

Together they went out into the street, lashed with slanting winter rains and crowded with lunch-hour shoppers hurrying by beneath umbrellas. Robyn led the way to a coffee lounge not far from the studio and they chose a table by a window.

"You know something? You've changed quite a bit since I saw you last!" His teasing glance rested on the pale composed face, the serious grey eyes. "If it hadn't been for the same old freckles –"

She wrinkled her nose at him. "Look who's talking!" She was thinking that during the years of absence he had altered almost beyond belief. He hadn't returned to New Zealand since going out to Fiji to claim his inheritance. The Johnny she remembered had been a tall gangling youth with a deprecating manner, but now ... He was heavier, broader. She noticed the muscles that rippled along the strong, darkly-tanned arms. The uncertain young man to whom she had bade goodbye at the wharf all those years ago was now a man, a Johnny-head-in-air. And what of herself? Did he see in her a self-sufficient young woman, at least to outward appearances, in place of the shy introspective art student?

As if tuned in on her line of thought he shot her a grin. "Four years can make a heck of a lot of difference! You never got around to coming out to see the old place?" Leaning forward, he extended a crumpled cigarette packet. "Why don't you make the trip out there, Rob? It's not what you'd call five-star accommodation exactly, but it's somewhere to put up." He held a flame to her cigarette, then his own. "Or is there some guy here that you just can't bear to tear yourself away from?"

"No, nothing like that."

He laughed. "You sound pretty definite about it."

"Oh, I am! There almost was, once or twice last year, but they fizzled out in the end."

"Not too much damage done?"

Laughingly she met his gaze. "None at all! My own fault really, I guess. I keep on expecting too much of people, then when they let me down, as they usually do in the end, I get horribly disappointed."

He nodded. "You always were a funny little kid. A tiger for loyalty, with a positive talent for wasting your affection on the wrong people!" He sent her a wry grin. "Don't overdo the pedestal thing with me, will you, Rob? It won't work!"

"Oh, I know *you*!" Her tone was affectionate, utterly confident. "It's so good to see you." The soft eager tones rushed on. "When did you get here? How long can you stay?"

"It's just a quick trip this time, I'm afraid. I've got to zip back in a hurry. Just came over to pick up some rigging for a schooner I'm interested in. I wanted to have a word with you, put you in the picture about how things are going over in Fiji, financially, that is. What I'm trying to say," a serious note threaded the light tones, "well, I guess you must have been wondering about the funds lately from the old place – or the lack of them?"

"Oh, that . . ." For the regular half-yearly cheques from the lawyer in Fiji had dwindled steadily over the past two years. But she had known it wouldn't be Johnny's fault that profits were now so small, almost non-existent. He would be doing his best. "Well," she said lightly, "it doesn't matter so much now that I've got a job, but I was awfully grateful for those remittances all the time I was at art school. I just couldn't have managed without them."

18

Leaning back in his chair, he studied her through a screen of cigarette smoke. "I might have known."

"What do you mean?"

"Oh, just that you'd take after the old man. One of us was bound to want to go around splashing paint on to canvas, like him! Boy, was he keen! You should see the place out at the coast! Daubs of local scenery hanging on every wall in the house and canvases by the dozen stacked outside in the shed. Not that I blame the old man altogether. Colour isn't just colour out there, it's extravagant, flamboyant, unbelievable! You've simply got to come out to the old Islander and see for yourself!"

"The Islander? I'd forgotten the name of the guesthouse –"

"If you could call it a guesthouse." He gave a short bitter laugh. "The old wreck's just about paying its way nowadays and that's all!"

"Oh dear," she put the worrying thought into words. "How do you manage about the staff . . . I mean, their wages?"

A shrug of broad shoulders. "Labour's cheap out in my part of the world, and they're a good crowd. I'm lucky enough to have a first-class helper, a woman who fills in for me while I'm away. Eve, Mrs. Daley, she'll be on the job now. She's been at the place for years, even when Dad was alive."

"But how about all the other expenses?"

"Oh, I get along. There are swags of fish just waiting to be netted in the bay. Food's cheap at the markets in Suva and tropical fruit trees grow wild around the place." He waved his cigarette carelessly. "Coconuts, paw-paw, bananas, all that stuff."

"All the same, it must be an awful struggle to keep the place going?"

"Not too bad. Most weeks I can pick up the odd dollar on the side. Often there's a trading schooner on the look-out for a crew or the odd photographer or tourist wanting someone to act as guide on a boat trip around the islands. That's about it, except for the coral boat. That brings in a bit, when I'm around to take her out."

19

"Coral boat?"

He nodded. "Didn't I tell you? She went with the place at the time when I took over years ago. Not a bad old tub, the *Katrina* —"

"Katrina! That was Mother's name."

"I know." The laughter died out of his face. "From what I've heard along the Coral Coast, Dad never bothered with women after they parted. You don't ever think of parents as people somehow, do you? You never know ... never will know now ... Oh well ..."

"Why do you call her the coral boat?"

"Wake up, Rob! That's what she is. She was specially built for the purpose of coral viewing. She's got glass observation panels along the bottom so that passengers can get a good view of what's going on down there below the coral reef."

She gazed at him entranced. "Do you take her out much?"

He threw her a rueful grin. "Too much for my liking! Dad used to make a bit extra that way to keep him going when the guesthouse was operating. When I came along I carried on with it. Then when they built the new top-luxury hotel around the point the South Pacific guests wanted to come along too. They arrive in a mini-bus and I take them out over the reef, tell them all about the fish and coral and marine life. It's a drag, but it brings in a little extra cash. Tell you what — why don't you come out and stay awhile, six months, a year! You could take over the running of the coral boat."

"But I wouldn't know a thing about it! You were the one who was brought up in Auckland where every back yard has a boat of some sort pulled up behind the house. I only wish I could sail a boat —"

"You can make up for it now! Come out to the old Islander and I'll show you how in three easy lessons. You'd pick it up in no time at all. Ever taken the controls of a motor boat?"

She shook her head. "I told you, you were the one who lived within sound of the sea."

"Nothing to it. I'll show you. It only brings in a few dollars a week," he murmured negligently, "but at least it's regular. They tell me that years ago when Dad first took it over the old Islander was quite a place, never without a crowd staying and every room booked in advance, but that was before Fiji started to put itself on the tourist map in a big way! Now the big resort hotels have got everything laid on. Poor old Dad, at the time he made out the will he probably thought he was leaving us something worthwhile. Maybe it was a paying outfit then, but now, let's face it, it's nothing but a rundown old place on the coast road. Oh, a great location, I grant you, bang on the water's edge with a terrific potential, but what it needs is to be updated. It's crying out for a pool, modern furnishings, a decent system of air conditioning, proper plumbing. All that would cost a packet! But I've got an idea, one that's going to solve all our financial problems. You see, Rob," he leaned forward, his grey eyes alight with enthusiasm, his voice tinged with excitement, "this brainwave of mine is a real money-spinner and if I can swing it, believe me, our money troubles will be over for good!"

She regarded him with questioning eyes as he swept on. "I've managed to raise enough cash to buy myself a share in a schooner. She's a beaut, one of the finest craft in her class I've ever come across and just the ticket for what we want her for. I've got a crew all jacked up. I'm the skipper and two of my mates who helped put up the money to buy her are in it too. We'll sign on a couple of Fijian boys as well."

"But how –"

"Oh, there'll be plenty of ways to make her pay for herself once we get her fitted up. One thing I've got in mind is making regular trips out to the islands lying just off the coast. The overseas promotions are putting up real tourist attractions on these little islands. They've built restaurants, provided boats for the use of guests. You can live quite cheaply and comfortably in a bure –"

"What's a bure?"

"It's a native hut thatched with coconut palm. You can

put up in one, fish, collect shells, explore the reefs, swim in the lagoon; stay for a day, a week, a month and really get the feeling of the islands. Thing is, the time's just right now for someone to provide more regular boat services, and guess who's going to do it! All I have to do now is to settle up the legal details for the purchase of the schooner with a guy in Wellington, and we'll be in business! There are lots of other ways we can make ourselves useful with the boat out there too," he ran on enthusiastically. "We'll be in the market for trading around the islands, picking up supplies of copra, coconut, bananas ... what have you. There's always a lot doing in that line. When everything's tied up legally we're going to take her for a few weeks' cruise around the islands, just to see how she makes out." He grinned. "Well, that's the excuse for giving ourselves a holiday!"

"Good luck, then! I hope it's a big success!"

"Don't worry, it will be!"

She'd always envied her brother his confidence in his own powers to carry out any scheme to which he set his mind.

"We can't miss! But that's no reason why you shouldn't make the trip out and stay at the coast any old time." As she glanced down at her wristwatch and began to gather up handbag and umbrella, he went on persuasively, "It won't make any difference to you! I'll be back to the house in between trips, wherever I happen to be, and you'll be okay with Mrs. Daley. She'll look after you. Might be an idea to wait until August, though, when the weather's right and the trade winds cool things down a bit."

When they were back at the door of the studio he pushed into her hand a sealed envelope. "Your share in advance of the profits to come! Why don't you use it for a trip over to the Islander? It's about time!"

"But I can't take this —"

"You will, you know! It's yours and I'm not arguing about it!" A tanned hand raised to his forehead in a smiling gesture of farewell and he had gone, striding away into the rainswept street before she could make any further protest.

During the following week Robyn found that her meeting with Johnny had left her with a curious feeling of restlessness. It wasn't long before she made up her mind to resign from her job at the studio and take that trip to Fiji. What matter if her brother happened to be away on his trading schooner? She would wait in the guesthouse – *their* guesthouse – until he returned. But August . . . three whole months away. That was far too long to wait. She would go right now, leave winter behind her and fly into the sun.

With a start she came back to the present. Heavens, what was she thinking of, staying here dreaming when the bus was due to leave the hotel in a few minutes! Swiftly she spilled the contents of her overnight bag on to the mahogany bureau beside the single red hibiscus blossom lying there. A touch of waterproof mascara to her lashes, a smear of suntan lotion to arms and legs, then she thrust towel and swimsuit into the bag, snatched up mauve-tinted sunglasses and hurried towards the foyer. Soon she was purchasing a ticket that included in the cost transport to nearby Lautoka, a cruise on the *Seaspray* to Castaway Island and a Polynesian dinner there. "You're only just in time," the smiling young Fijian girl receptionist told her.

"You can give me one of those too!" Surely she recognised the pleasant accents. Startled, Robyn glanced over her shoulder to meet David Kinnear's smiling glance. It was such a heart-warming look that suddenly she was glad she had decided on this particular day cruise. To have a companion on the trip would make the outing even more enjoyable.

When he had purchased his ticket they strolled towards the entrance with its banks of climbing tropical greenery. Glancing towards the stack of luggage piled against the wall, she said, "I can see your name on the label of one of the bags."

He nodded. "I'm pushing off today. Then it's over to Suva for a couple of days before I begin work on the new job down the coast. And you're –"

"Oh, I'm staying the night here, then I'll be taking the bus to the Coral Coast in the morning."

"A good place to stay if you want to relax, sunbathe — where are you putting up?"

"Me? Oh, at the Islander." She was gazing around her at the patchwork of green. "All that sugar cane. I wonder which is the month when it's cut —"

"*The Islander!*" At the incredulous tone of his voice she glanced towards him in surprise.

"Why, what's wrong with that?"

But he had recovered himself and was saying evenly. "Nothing, nothing at all! It's comfortable enough, so they tell me — that is if you want to cut expenses and can put up with the old style of accommodation. It's certainly got a terrific situation, right on the beach. Anyway, you can always move on somewhere else if it doesn't suit you."

"I wouldn't want to go anywhere else!" At that moment a tourist bus moved up the concreted slope towards them and Robyn made her way out into the sunshine. David Kinnear followed her as she mounted the high steps of the air-conditioned vehicle, then seated himself at her side.

The windows afforded a wide view and she gazed eagerly ahead to the grassy green slopes with their perfumed tropical bushes. Presently they sped up a rise, then drew in at the entrance of an older type of guesthouse where a group stood waiting on an open verandah festooned in a blazing curtain of purple bougainvillaea. Soon they were moving along the road leading to the harbour, passing oxen grazing along the lush grass of the roadside. As they travelled in the shade of a long avenue of towering banyan trees with their trailing aerial roots, he said, "That's the one I was telling you about."

Laughing, she said, "Bula?"

"That's right. The timber the natives use for carving their masks and ornaments and models of tiny outrigger canoes. Only they've got their own name for the tree— 'Mother-in-law's tongue', they call it."

"I can guess why!" She had already noticed the long hang-

24

ing yellow seedpods hanging from the thickly-growing tangle of branches.

The next moment she was gazing ahead towards a native village. In a clearing among the trees was a cluster of thatched huts. Goats nibbled at the long grass. Further along the route, dark-eyed children, trudging along the dusty road, waved and smiled a greeting to the passengers in the tourist bus. Then they were running parallel with a narrow railway line. "Next month they'll cut the sugar cane," David told her, "and run it into the mill at Lautoka, the sugar town. They say it's the only free train ride in the world and the trip is quite an experience. You should have come along to Lautoka a bit later in the season."

"Who can tell? I may still be around here then."

"I might take you for a ride on it!"

"Talking about free rides . . ." Robyn's gaze was caught by a vividly coloured blue butterfly, its purple-veined wings outspread against the glass of the windscreen.

Presently they were passing through the clean spacious streets of the sugar town with its lush greenery, Indian temples and modern stores. Beyond, the line of blue peaks appeared so close Robyn felt she had merely to reach forward to touch them.

They turned towards the sea where motor vessels and yachts, schooners and catamarans rocked gently on calm waters. Leaning on the deck rail of the *Seaspray* as the schooner drew away from the wharf, Robyn eyed the mingled races gathered there – Indian family parties, the women with their glistening black hair and colourful flowing saris, groups of Fijians in their vividly printed sulus, a sprinkling of overseas tourists. Mist was rolling in over the mountain peaks and out here on the water the breeze had freshened, lightening the humidity of the atmosphere. She brought her gaze back to the deck and the smiling Fijian crew in their white "Seaspray" T-shirts splashed in a pattern of dark blue hibiscus blossoms.

"It's a bit like finding yourself in the middle of a Cinemascope scene," she told the man at her side. For in the distance small islands floated in a blue haze on the horizon. Near at hand a palm-fringed atoll, ringed with white sand, rose like a mirage from dark blue-green water.

Further along the deck a group of air crew, pilots and hostesses, were laughing and chatting together. Robyn however was content to stand quietly at the rail, watching the great wind-filled sails billowing overhead and the shower of spindrift flung up from the bows. An organza day! And having someone with whom to share it made everything just about perfect. She stole a glance towards her companion's averted profile. He'd be a shade over thirty, she would imagine, this burly dark man with an air of relaxation and a perceptive smile. Something about him gave her an impression of a man who had been everywhere, done everything, yet there was about him an air of disarming friendliness and she got an impression that he was enjoying the excursion today as much as she was. The thought prompted her to say idly: "I expect you've often made this trip?"

He turned to face her. "I've been out to a lot of the outlying islands by motor vessel, but never like this."

"You mean, not out to Castaway under sail?"

His gaze rested on the sensitive young face, the long strands of fair hair blowing around Robyn's eyes in the strong breeze. "I mean," there was an enigmatical expression in the dark eyes, "not like this."

"The same, only different," she twinkled up at him. "Like falling in love?"

"Something like that. You seem to know a lot about it," he observed in his deceptively quiet tones, "for nineteen —"

"And a half," she amended with dignity.

"And a half," he conceded with gravity, but she had caught a glimmer of amusement in his eyes.

"I'm not a child, you know," she said stiffly.

"I didn't say you were."

"No, but ... what I mean is ..." She was floundering wildly, regretting having allowed herself to stray into this dangerous territory with a man who was so much older and

26

more experienced than herself.

"Look, there's Castaway," he was saying, "you can just see it . . . over there!"

She followed his gaze towards a smudge of green in the distance. She had the absurd feeling that she would be quite content to sail on like this for ever beneath the bluest of blue skies with the wind singing in the rigging overhead and just for company, of course, David Kinnear at her side.

She soon realised, however, that the hazy island was further away than she had at first imagined and another hour had gone by before they approached it. Now she could discern a flat island thickly covered with clustered coconut palms, white sandy beaches, fringed by reefs. Boats were pulled up on the shore and natives on water-skis pulled by circling launches, skimmed by in a plume of spray.

Presently they were leaving the schooner, dropping down in to a small power boat while a Fijian crew guided them into the lagoon. Here the water was a pale turquoise in the shallows, a darker blue beyond the reefs. Robyn slipped off her scuffs and with David, waded ashore.

"Don't let the outside look of the bures fool you," he told her as they strolled up the wide expanse of sand and came in sight of thatched huts hidden amongst the coconut palms. "They might look primitive at first sight, but you'd be surprised to find how comfortable they are once you're inside. Fans, showers, refrigerators, everything you could wish for for easy living. That big one over there," she followed his gaze towards a large open-sided hut with coconut fibre thatched roofing, "is the restaurant." She took in the dotted tables and cane chairs, the long bar at one end of the open-air building. "Let's have a swim to cool off, shall we?"

She left him to make her way up a sandy track winding upwards amongst tall palms towards a rough signpost nailed to a tree trunk: "Women's Changing Shed". Once inside the thatched shed she discovered the truth of David's words, for whirring fans overhead kept the air cool and fresh and water flowed from porcelain basins and individual showers. In a partitioned section of the shelter she changed into her swim-suit, conscious of her pale skin from which last summer's tan had long since faded. But not for long, she promised herself, and went out to join the man waiting at the water's edge. Together they ran over thick sand, then plunged into limpid water. Never before had Robyn lingered for so long in the sea, but then never previously had she swum in water so warm and enticing. They circled rocks that shelved deeply out to the coral reef in a sea so clear they could see clearly down to the shells lying on the sand below. At last they waded out through the wavelets that were tossing a fringe of white lace on wet sand and leaving the cluster of bures behind them, strolled around a point. All at once there was nothing but sea and sand, no sound but the whisper of wind in the tall palms on the shore mingling with the soft murmuring of the waves. They threw themselves down on the sand and let the hot sun beat down on their backs. "It's like sugar," Robyn said, watching the thick grains of sand trickling through her fingers.

A little later she was roused from a dreamy sense of re-laxation by a muffled sound. She jerked her head upwards and pushed the long hair from her eyes. "Whatever's that?"

"Just a Fijian keeping up an ancient custom. He's beating a tattoo on a lali drum, a hollow log, giving us the message that it's time to roll up for an island dinner. Are you ready for it?"

"I'm famished! It must be all this sea air!" They rose and made their leisurely way along the beach, following a broken line of shells and coral. When they came in sight of the bay Robyn saw that long tables were set in the shade of spreading trees and smoke was rising from fires where barbecued steaks were being prepared by natives, bare to the waist, in their skirt-like cotton sulus.

At intervals along the leaf-covered tables, flower-garlanded native girls were serving food piled in great white conch shells to a long line of guests. There were steaming curries, sizzling steaks, rice, an assortment of green salads, sweetcorn, wafer-thin bread. Piled mounds of tropical fruits – golden paw-

paw, pineapple, bananas – were set between massive bowls of glowing hibiscus blossoms and pink and white coral from the reef. There were cans of Australian beer and chilled lemonade.

Robyn thought the meal was delightful. "And we don't even have to clear up afterwards," she told David as they moved towards bamboo seats set in the shade of the trees and facing the sea.

"Oh, the staff don't have to work too hard. There's no shortage of labour here and they'll soon whip through the plates. Besides, they've got a special arrangement, not a human one, that takes care of all the food scraps left lying about. Watch and you'll see what I mean –"

"I don't believe it!"

"No, honestly, look over there! No, thisaway, up the track!" A hand pressed gently to her cheek, he turned her face towards the tables under the trees where Fijian girls were gathering up plates and cutlery. For a moment she had difficulty in concentrating on the scene before her, for David Kinnear's touch had affected her in the oddest way, making her feel so terribly ... *aware* of him. A man she scarcely knew, a stranger. She couldn't understand herself, and to cover her confusion she stared determinedly in the direction he had indicated. The next moment she burst into laughter. It was so unexpected, for as at a given signal, down the winding sandy pathway swaggered a line of plump white turkeys. On reaching the clearing where the tables were set, they proceeded to gobble up each scrap of food left lying on the sand. Then, with the same orderly precision that had marked their arrival, they turned and moved back up the slope to disappear from view a few moments later amongst the trees.

"Well," she gazed towards him laughingly, "next time I'll believe you!"

"I'll hold you to that, one of these days!" For a moment an odd unreadable expression flitted across his face. It was almost, she told herself perplexedly, as though he suspected something concerning her, something of which she was in ignorance. But how could that be? Really, he was the most puzzling, intriguing of men, yet she liked him, she liked him a lot! It's just the spell of the islands working, she jeered at herself.

If only the sun-drenched day wasn't flying by so swiftly. A stroll around the island, which wasn't very large, then it was time to join the crowd who were converging at the restaurant and straggling down the beach. In a heap on the sand were piled travel bags and suitcases belonging to the holiday-makers who had enjoyed an extended period of rest and relaxation in this most relaxing of islands.

Presently they were climbing aboard a small motor boat and to the sound of farewells shouted from the Fijian crew, they drew away from Castaway and moved in the direction of the white-sailed schooner beyond the reef. On board the *Seaspray* the waving figures on the island receded as the craft swept over an inky-blue sea and the trade winds blew cool and soft on their sun-flushed faces.

Around them guitars plucked by a singing Fijian crew throbbed in the age-old melodies of the South Pacific. Before long everyone on board joined in the haunting rhythm, as the wind-filled sails bore them back towards the jungle-clad mountain peaks ahead, now wreathed in moist grey clouds.

As they neared their destination strumming guitars fell into the haunting strains of the traditional Fijian song of farewell. Even as far away as New Zealand, Robyn had been familiar with the strains of "Isa Lei" and now both she and David joined in the words of the poignant melody.

They were still singing as the *Seaspray* glided in towards the dark waters of the wharves. Idly Robyn's gaze swept over the crowd gathered there, then all at once she stiffened.

"Johnny!" Her excited cry cut across the thrumming guitars and chorus of voices. He caught her eye, then to her surprise he swung around on his heel and was lost to sight amongst the throng. The hand she had lifted in greeting dropped to her side. It *had* been him, his jaunty grin and sun-tanned features, a yachting cap perched at a rakish angle over

30

one eye. She *couldn't* have made a mistake. Nor had there been the slightest doubt regarding his initial glance of recognition. He had looked delighted to catch sight of her, surprised but delighted, then his glance had moved towards her companion and immediately he had vanished. She stared after him bewilderedly. "Oh ... he's gone!" She scarcely realised she was speaking her thoughts aloud. "Now why would he do a thing like that?" All at once she realised that David was regarding her attentively.

"Do what?" For all his smile was so beguiling she was aware of a shade of watchfulness in his expression.

"Run away. Johnny saw me, I know he did! Just for a moment his whole face lighted up. You know? Then he rushed away in the crowd just as though he didn't want to see me."

"Your brother is Johnny Carlisle?" His voice was low and contained, yet there was an intent look in his dark eyes that puzzled her. She turned and faced him. "Why, yes, do you know him?"

"No, not really."

There it was again, the sudden tightening of his expression that faintly disturbed her, made her feel uneasy, almost ... apprehensive. "Let's just say," his cool unresponsive tone was in such marked contrast to his lazy accents that she stared back at him in surprise, "that I've run across him once or twice, in business."

The crowd of disembarking passengers surged around them as they made their way in the wake of the straggling line moving in the direction of the gangplank. Robyn's searching glance darted over the cosmopolitan throng, hoping to catch a glimpse of a tall figure, a bronzed face beneath a yachting cap, but of course he wasn't there. He had gone, goodness knows why! Perhaps, she comforted herself, she had merely imagined his brief look of recognition. At least she knew that Johnny was here on the island of Vita Levu and not away at sea in his oceangoing craft.

She moved with David towards a waiting bus standing

amongst the cluster of vehicles on the wharf, but in the crowd they were separated. It was not until they stood together in the foyer of the hotel and he moved towards the stack of travel bags that she realised she wouldn't be seeing him again. Not that she minded – now, for he was wearing his curious closed look again, just as though there had been no memorable day spent together on a South Pacific island. She was conscious of a throng of tourists milling around them and the fleet of taxis waiting at the entrance.

"Don't look like that," he chided, "you're in the Happy Isles, the Land of Endless Summer. Remember?"

She summoned a smile and made an effort to push aside the sudden desolate feeling of being alone in a strange land that had swept over her. "Well, thanks for the company on the cruise. It was great."

"Made all the difference to me too."

She broke the uncomfortable silence with a forced laugh. "I might run across you one of these days, somewhere between here and there on the Coral Coast."

"That's right." He too appeared constrained and strangely ill at ease. David Kinnear, whom she would have imagined to be the last man on earth to feel such an emotion, much less betray it. "See you again, maybe. That is," once again the unfathomable expression crossed his face, "if you're still interested by then."

A Fijian taxi-driver was approaching and David picked up his travel bag and turned away. He didn't even look back, Robyn thought forlornly. He'd just ... gone ... with that cryptic reference to her not wishing to see him again when next they met – whatever that might mean. She sighed and moved slowly across the crowded reception room. Maybe it was as well that their friendship had ended almost before it had begun. Better not to get involved with a man who, for some reason, appeared determined to keep her at arm's length, who said things that didn't make sense, and who, let's face it, attracted her even against her will.

CHAPTER II

THERE were few passengers on the bus bound for the dusty Queens Road that skirted the Coral Coast. Robyn gazed out of the window, her idle glance resting on a nearby field where a Fijian youth guided a plough drawn by sturdy oxen. The scarlet tassels of the spreading flame tree blazed against a blue sky and frangipani, perfuming the air with its fragrance, grew wild at the edges of the road and bordered the sweeping driveways that led up to the various tourist hotels and guesthouses at which the vessel paused in order to pick up passengers.

Presently they entered the small township of Nandi. Taxis hooted wildly around them and the narrow streets were lined with small dark shops. Indian store-keepers stood waiting in entrances while overseas tourists made their selection from the display windows crowded with radios, tape-recorders and stereos at this last opportunity to purchase duty-free goods at bargain prices before leaving the country from the adjacent airport.

Then they were out in the open once more, passing two small Fijian boys who were bumping along the rough ride astride a horse. Now the yellow dust was rising in clouds around the windows. Already Robyn could feel the gritty taste in her mouth, but still she gazed out entranced as they took undulating hills, dipping down to the vivid green of rice fields, then swooping up to meet clouds lying low over the hills ahead. In a clearing by the roadside she glimpsed a tiny schoolroom. Was this where the lads on horseback were bound? The next moment her attention was captured by a roadside stall heaped high with melons, bananas, pineapples. At intervals, through a fringe of palms she caught glimpses of blue of the coast, then lost them as the vehicle ground on towards hills clothed in luxuriant jungle, narrowly missing Indian men riding bicycles and horses meandering across the path. In spite of the discomfort, the dust, the heat, she was enjoying the ride. Not as much as she would have done had David Kinnear been with her on the journey up the coast, but still . . . Would she ever see him again? If so — her wide mouth quirked at the corners — it would certainly be only by chance, for he had shown no special desire to further their acquaintance, in spite of the pleasure he had seemed to take in her company. Unconsciously she sighed, then brought her mind back to the present as the lurching vehicle followed the curving line of the coast. Waves were creaming in over reefs and tall palms growing along the water's edge bent to meet the mirrored reflections in limpid lagoons.

"Anyone for the Islander?" The driver's call brought her to instant awareness and gathering up shoulder bag and camera she made her way to the door. The next moment she found herself on a dusty road, her shabby suitcase at her feet, in what appeared to her to be the middle of a tropical nowhere with the warm blue Pacific ocean on one side of her and on the other, a screen of tall coconut palms. Feeling increasingly conscious of the heat, she trudged along in the dust of the road, peering through the greenery. At last with a sense of relief she glimpsed a timber building almost concealed by tall feathery date palms. The long low bungalow showed no evidence of life, but as she went up the steps of the verandah running the width of the house, a man carrying a fishing rod appeared around a corner of the building.

"Rob!" For a moment Johnny stood transfixed, then he hurried towards her. "Where on earth did you spring from?"

She laughed and waited for him to reach the top step. "American Airlines, actually, two days ago. I thought I'd stay on for an extra day in Nandi. Your fault — I fell for one of those sea excursions to the outlying islands by schooner that you told me about. I thought you'd be surprised to see me."

"Surprised isn't the word for it! Come on inside — no, wait, it's cooler out here on the verandah. There's something we've got to get straightened out."

Could it be the moist enervating heat, she wondered, that

was beading his bronzed forehead with perspiration? Why was he looking so . . . so strained, like a man with something on his mind? A pang of apprehension shot through her, but she made herself smile, say lightly, "You know, the funniest thing happened yesterday. I thought I saw you among the crowd on the wharf at Lautoka –"

He brushed her words aside with an impatient gesture. "Never mind about that. Look, Rob, there are things you should know." She could barely catch the low words. "Thing is, I've had a spot of trouble."

"What's wrong? Girl trouble?" she said teasingly.

"Not exactly, though that comes into it too. I had the idea that if I could only hang on for a while something would turn up, something to tide me over a bad patch, but as things turned out, the only thing that turned up was Kinnear, damn him!"

"Kinnear!" she echoed blankly. "Oh," enlightenment dawned on her, "now I get it! That was why you didn't want to recognise me on the wharf yesterday. I *knew* you'd seen me –"

"Oh, I saw you all right. It really threw me, seeing you standing there on the deck of the *Seaspray* with *him*. We'll be seeing enough of him as it is. More than enough," he added in a low tone.

Her clear gaze swept up to meet his downcast look. "Don't you like him?"

"*Like him?* Look here, we'd better have this out right now before we go any further," his wry grin didn't reach his eyes, "put you in the picture about Kinnear. Didn't he let on to you about me? I should have thought he'd have been only too pleased to rub it in!"

"You know," she murmured bewilderedly, "I haven't the slightest idea what you're talking about."

"I'll tell you. You'll get the news from someone else pretty soon anyway. A lot's been happening out here since I saw you last, Rob. Kinnear, he's taking over here. He's the boss. Do you understand? You and me, we won't count that much!"

35

He snapped his fingers angrily.

She stared at him. "You mean you've sold the guesthouse to David Kinnear?"

"I wish to heaven I had," he groaned. "No, it's a grimmer outlook than that! You see, it's the money. You remember I told you I borrowed fairly heavily to buy a share in the schooner?"

"Borrowed? But I thought you had the money –"

"Well, maybe I didn't make it plain. I forget. Anyway, it's too late now. The bloke I owe the money to is Kinnear. Now do you see how it is? When the schooner was wrecked –"

She stared at him aghast. "But you didn't tell me –"

He glanced evasively away. "I meant to write, but anyway it doesn't make any difference now. First week out," he went on moodily, "and she hit a coral reef, holed the side and there wasn't a chance of getting her off. Some natives on one of the islands saw what had happened and came out in outriggers to rescue us. A week later a ship called, picked us up and brought us back to Suva."

"But wasn't there insurance?"

He shrugged the question away. "Not enough to make much difference. After that I hadn't much choice in what happened. What could I do but go to the lawyer in town and tell him the sad story? We had a meeting, the boat owners, the lawyer and Kinnear, and the upshot of it all was that Kinnear came up with the bright idea of rearranging the mortgage, and seeing there wasn't a chance of paying back the original money we'd borrowed or even the interest on it, now that the schooner's gone for good, he'd make me another loan –"

"That was decent of him."

"*Decent of him?*" He gave a brief hard laugh. "Don't fool yourself about Kinnear, Rob. He didn't do it for me. It was the only way he could think of to retrieve any of his cash. On *his* terms, of course. He has all the say. Seeing the old place happens to have such a great location, bang on the beach, handy to an airstrip, he reckons to put up the money on the understanding – wait for it – that he's to be given a free hand in updating the whole outfit. He plans to change everything, put in a pool, new plumbing, modern air conditioning, alter the whole layout, make the old Islander into a paying proposition in line with the other resort places that are springing up all along the coast."

"But we're still the owners . . . aren't we?"

Once again he gave that short bitter laugh. "Oh yes, we're the owners, and a fat lot of good that will do us! You can see for yourself the position he's put us in. Now he can do just what he likes with the place, and that goes for you and me too. Sorry, Sis, but I guess I've signed the Islander over to him. But what else could I do? It'll be great, won't it, having him hanging around the place all the time, throwing his weight about, telling me what to do with my own property! I can stay on as manager, he says. Big deal! You know, just talking to him makes me nervous. He's so darn smiling and friendly, then wham! Out of the blue he comes up with something like this. Make no mistake, he knows what he's doing, and we can't do anything but play along with him. I'm not so sure that I can stick it!" He turned towards her a dark resentful glance. "What on earth made you latch on to him, of all people, on the schooner?"

"It was just . . . we were both staying at Travelodge – "She checked herself and thought better of the eager confidences she had been about to pour out. "He happened to be going on the Castaway Island cruise too. Oh, it was all right," she assured him quickly, "he didn't know who I was. I just told him my name was Robyn, that was all."

"All?" All at once she realised the significance of David Kinnear's speculative glance when she had mentioned her brother. Now she knew why the sense of happy comradeship between them had evaporated from that moment. He had suspected all along who she was, she was certain of it, and her mention of Johnny had confirmed her identity beyond all doubt. Writhing inwardly, she heard her own voice saying lightly, boastfully, *stupidly* it must have seemed to him, "I've got a share in some property here." Oh, that really must have amused him. No wonder he had regarded her with that cryptic smile of his. All the time he had been laughing at her.

Aloud she murmured, "It wasn't your fault that you struck trouble out on the reef and lost the boat." To herself she added, If only it wasn't David Kinnear who's taking everything over. She put into the words the question that plucked at her mind. "When is he coming to see about starting the alterations?"

"Tomorrow." Johnny spoke through clenched lips.

She gathered herself together and spoke with more cheerfulness than she felt. "Well, at least we'll be here together."

He didn't appear to have heard her. "Don't be taken in by that friendly manner of his. He's like that to everyone! Underneath it all he's right out to collect his pound of flesh! And we can't do a thing about it! I've signed over the place – well, fair enough! But if he thinks he can make me into his runabout man ... Just let him start trying to push me around – or you!" His brooding glance rested on Robyn's troubled face.

"Don't worry," she said, "I can look after myself!"

He flung his half-smoked cigarette into the bushes below. "You'd better come inside, take a look around. Choose a room for yourself," he added with heavy sarcasm, "while you can take your pick and before Kinnear begins pulling the whole show to pieces and putting it together again – his way!" He turned to pick up her modest suitcase. "Hope you brought some mosquito repellent with you?"

She nodded. "I picked up that much information on my way here."

He kicked open a screen door and they moved into a long dark passage with rooms opening off it on either side. "See what I mean?" He paused to fling open a bedroom door, then another, where there was nothing but the empty shabby rooms, the enervating heat.

Robyn wiped her moist forehead with her handkerchief. "I can hear voices," she whispered. "Someone's in the room opposite."

38

He nodded, leading her past a closed door. "Old faithfuls — a couple of elderly blokes. It's the informal atmosphere here that's the attraction, so they say. Informal's right! The few odd fishermen turn up each season too. It's handy to the fishing grounds, and cheap living. You'll see them —" He stopped short as a door at the end of the hallway opened and a small dark girl stood facing them, trim and attractive in her blue air hostess uniform.

"Hi, Pam!" Johnny looked taken aback. Clearly Robyn thought he hadn't known that the other girl was in the house. "I wasn't expecting to see you this weekend."

"I didn't know I was coming here myself until the last minute before the plane left. I got last-minute orders to change with another hostess on the Fiji flight. We got in at midnight. Nice surprise?" Sparkling dark eyes challenged him and Robyn was aware of an unmistakable current of feeling flowing between the other two. If Johnny had fallen in love with this nice dark girl at least luck couldn't be all against him!

"Pam," he was saying, "my sister Robyn."

"Your sister?" The other girl's eyes seemed to leave his face with an effort. "I didn't know you had one."

Robyn smiled. "It's true. Not that I see much of him, but that's something I intend to put right, here on the coast."

"I can see the resemblance now," Pam said slowly. "You two do look a lot like brother and sister."

"Actually," Robyn told her ruefully, "We're more like distant relations, very distant. We only see each other every few years or so."

"Well, I'm off to change out of this uniform and get into something cooler, more in line with the South Pacific image. See you later, Johnny." It seemed to Robyn that the dark eyes were pleading, but the man made no effort to detain her and she turned away.

Robyn looked after her. She had taken an immediate liking to this small sturdy-looking girl with an air of vitality. "She's nice," she volunteered as they strolled on down the passage.

"Oh, Pam's okay." Apparently Johnny was disinclined to enlarge on the subject of the vivacious-looking air hostess. Yet Robyn got an impression that there was something deeper than mere friendship between the two. Perhaps they had quarrelled. She forgot the matter as she entered a large dining room with coconut matting on the floor. Small bamboo tables were set with woven fibre mats and above her head a large revolving fan stirred the humid atmosphere.

"Here she is, Eve! My sister Robyn I was telling you about."

"Oh, hello!" A middle-aged woman who had been bending over an office desk turned and stepped towards them. She wore a cool loose frock of crisp cotton patterned in a native design. Robyn saw a keen-eyed woman with neat short-cropped grey hair, a deeply tanned skin – and a smile that was warm with welcome. "If only you'd let us know you were on your way, we would have gone in to the airport and collected you. Has Johnny shown you over the place yet?"

"Oh yes, thank you. He's –" She stopped short, her attention caught by the vivid flame, orange and apricot shadings of an oil painting hanging on the opposite wall. Pushing a damp lock of hair back from her flushed forehead, she moved across the room and looked up towards the sunset scene.

"The fans aren't very efficient," Mrs. Daley apologised, "but they're better than nothing. Yes, that's one of your father's paintings." She came to stand at Robyn's side. "What do you think of it?"

"It's certainly ... colourful." That at least was the truth. She could scarcely voice her opinion that much as her father must have enjoyed his hobby, this wasn't the work of a professional painter. Far from it. The garish colours ... and the perspective ...

"He loved painting sunsets," the older woman was saying, "they fascinated him."

Robyn asked gently, "Did he sell any of his pictures?"

"Oh no! He always said he couldn't bear to part with one of them!"

"You knew him well, then?"

"My goodness, yes! I've been at the Islander for years and years. Andrew and I used to run the place together."

"What was he like, Mrs. Daley? I mean, what sort of a man was he?"

"Oh, a bit of a dreamer, not very practical when it came to managing money. Things like that. But I was able to give him a hand there. At least the place used to pay its own way with a little bit over in those days. That was before the tourist boom hit Fiji. Nowadays tourists can choose between any number of luxury resorts on the islands. But we still have a few regulars who turn up each season, thank heaven. And once David Kinnear gets going on making the alterations here, things will be very different! They say he's the top man in architecture in Fiji, with an international reputation in his own line and a real flair for the designing of new complexes. He's quite gifted too, I believe, when it comes to interior design. All the overseas travel promoters are rushing to sign him up to design their new world-class hotels." Her voice rang with enthusiasm. "I do think Johnny had all the luck in the world in managing to get him to do over the old Islander!"

Robyn reflected that it was fortunate that this cheerful woman hadn't caught the sardonic twist of her brother's lips. She brought her mind back to the clear tones.

"Once he's modernised it and arranged the decoration and furnishings, everything will be different! Just the fact of his having had the commission for the work will be recommendation enough for the travel agents and tourist heads. They tell me that once he starts work on a place, he doesn't lose any time. Gets the plans drawn up and workmen started on the job right away!" She turned a bright face towards Johnny. "Can you believe that in just a few months we'll be on top again, the place crowded with tourists, and all the improvements we've always wanted but never thought we'd get. A decent system of air-conditioning, a big swimming pool in front of the house, an open-air restaurant where we can put

41

on island dinners and entertainments. We were awfully fortunate to get his services. I mean, a man like David Kinnear."

Johnny muttered something unintelligible. So his loyal helper had no idea of the true position regarding the changes to be made in the guesthouse, Robyn mused, or the fact that Johnny had no choice in the matter of renovations. At his dark expression she half expected him to break into an angry tirade. She laid a hand on his brown arm. "How about this tour of inspection we're on?"

He swung towards her. "We're on our way. See you at lunch, Eve."

When they had seen the big old kitchen where Fijian youths were busily preparing salads and cold meats at a long table in the centre of the room, Johnny led the way towards the bathrooms, then moved out of a door into brilliant sunshine. He waved a careless hand towards a cluster of outbuildings. "You wouldn't be interested in anything there. There're just storage sheds, somewhere to keep the deep freeze, odds and ends, nothing you'd want to see."

"But I do! Didn't you say that some of Dad's pictures were out there?"

"Some! If you're going to go through that lot you'll be here for the rest of the day." He pushed open a rickety door and she peered into the dimness of a cluttered timber shed. "There you are, stacked against the wall, dozens of them. They're all yours! Help yourself!"

Eagerly Robyn bent to pick up a large canvas. She blew away a film of dust and stood looking down at a portrait of a Fijian warrior in all his glory of hair ornaments, long earrings and war paint. Still she could find little merit in her father's work, which seemed to her not to have progressed beyond a certain stage of development. Perhaps he hadn't realised it himself; she hoped not. Carefully she flicked over one canvas after another, then at last she propped the stack of paintings back against the wall.

Outside, a hairy brown coconut was lying on the lush

green grass and she glanced around her at the closely-growing coconut palms, long fringed banana leaves; papaya, the great yellow fruit half eaten by the myriad birds flying overhead amongst the tropical growth. Then they were following a twisting path, passing bushes of flowering hibiscus with their brilliant yellow, red and pink blossoms. Suddenly they came on a line of thatched huts, half hidden amidst thick greenery. Doors opened on to an overgrown concrete terrace. Robyn paused. "Who sleeps in these?"

"No one uses them much. In the old days Eve used to put the overflow from the house out in the bures, so she tells me. Like to sleep out here yourself, instead of up at the house? They've got fans, of a sort, and the windows are meshed against mosquitoes."

"Oh, I would!" She was enchanted with the small native-style dwellings. Sleeping in one of these she would be close to the beach, hear the surge of breakers pounding ceaselessly against the reef. With all the flowers and perfume around her it would be like living in the centre of a garden. "I'll move in today! What's along at the end of the path?"

He shrugged. "Nothing much. The path leads to a native village a couple of miles away. It's just a sort of bush walk."

On the way back to the house they were met by a tall, big-framed Fijian girl in a long printed sulu that swirled around brown ankles. She smiled shyly towards Robyn. "*Bula*."

On this occasion Robyn could return the greeting without self-consciousness. At least this was something David Kinnear had taught her. The way things had turned out, she couldn't imagine their ever being as friendly as on that unforgettable day out at Castaway Island. Now being forced to meet him again under such different circumstances promised to be a strain, an ordeal she was already coming to dread.

"Selani," Johnny was saying, "this is my sister Robyn. She's come to stay for a while and she likes the idea of living in a bure. Get one fixed up for her, will you? One of the end ones will do."

The Fijian girl nodded shyly, her soft brown eyes under a

crop of curly dark hair, fixed on Robyn. Then, moving with her erect and graceful carriage, she left them. A little later a native youth carried Robyn's suitcase into the thatched hut. The room was immaculately clean with fresh cotton spreads covering twin beds and fluffy dry towels on a rack by the basin. On a low bamboo table was set a flask of iced water and a great white seashell filled with vividly-shaded hibiscus blossoms.

Left alone, Robyn moved to the louvre windows and stood peering out into the cluster of tropical trees and perfumed blossoming shrubs. Banana leaves swished in the breeze, their branches drooping with their burden of incredibly large russet-coloured flowers. In her ears the soft wash of the waves on the sand nearby merged with the whirring of the fans. It was all warm and tropical and delightful – and it belonged – well, near enough to make no difference, to David Kinnear!

Thrusting the disquieting thought aside, she set about hanging the gay cotton tops and short frocks in the wardrobe, stowing make-up and sun-tan lotions in a drawer in the shabby chest. A quick wash, then she changed her linen shift for a loose cotton frock printed in a design of native birds, that she had purchased at the gift shop in the hotel at Nandi. There was no doubt that the vivid peacock-blue shadings did something for her, she told her reflection in the fly-speckled mirror. The splashes of brilliant colour contrasted with her dark-blonde hair and lent colour to her eyes. All she needed now to complete the picture was a Pacific-island tan, and at least that was one acquisition here that was free for the taking and had nothing at all to do with David Kinnear.

When she returned to the house a midday meal was being served in the dining room. Mrs. Daley took her to a table at the end of the room. "Johnny'll be along at any moment."

As Robyn glanced around her she reflected that the place was certainly badly in need of attention. It had the run-down air of a guesthouse that was on the way down. If only she and Johnny could have pulled it together between them. If

44

only they weren't totally dependent on the services of David Kinnear!

Her gaze moved over the scattered tables with their sprinkling of guests. A family party were seated not far away – mother, father and three small boys, who by their pale appearance were evidently not yet familiar with the hot Pacific sun. Nearby were seated two middle-aged women, probably escaping New Zealand's mild winter season. A group of older men, bronzed and rugged-looking types, shared a table and fragments of their conversation reached her. Their talk was of big game fishing, of record catches of previous years, of tides and reefs.

"Mind if I join you?" The air hostess who she had met earlier in the day paused beside her.

"Of course not." Even the one brief upward glance had told Robyn that the other girl's eyes were swollen with weeping.

Pam chatted gaily, but all the time her glance went to the open doorway. Yet when at last Johnny did appear the two seemed to have nothing to say to each other. Robyn found herself wondering once again about the involvement between the small dark girl and her brother.

When the meal was over and two Fijian house-girls began to clear away the dishes, Johnny turned to Robyn. "Like to have a run out in the boat and see the coral gardens?"

She raised shining eyes. "Would I ever! It's one of the things I've been looking forward to ever since you told me about it."

"Right. We'll take off down to the beach." As an afterthought he turned to Pam. "How about you, Pam?"

"No, thanks, Johnny. I've been there before." Yet she was looking at him, Robyn thought, as though he were her whole world. What was the trouble between these two?

Presently, however, as she waded out through the shallows towards the flat-bottomed motor boat rocking gently on a calm sea, Robyn forgot everything else in the enjoyment of the moment. Soon they were cutting through the water as they

45

sped towards the line of white surf curling over the reef. As they dropped speed and glided over the coral reef Robyn gazed down through the glass panels to a wonderland of colour far below the swaying seaweeds. Fascinated, she watched as they glided over green seagrass and moss-filled caverns. At times the boat seemed to scrape the coral, then they would be above shadowy cliffs, shelving away hundreds of feet below. A shoal of tiny striped tiger-fish drifted by in the cloudy blue depths, followed by darting angel-fish that seemed to Robyn like a cluster of coloured butterflies. Johnny cut the engine and they drifted on the waves. The sun shone on the water and each moment disclosed a fresh sight in the underwater gardens. A bright violet fish slid across her vision and the clusters of pink and wine-red spreading ever upwards reminded Robyn of the blossoming plants in New Zealand gardens, but these flowers were coral formations, slowly growing in the sun-warmed waters of the reef.

The lazy sense of relaxation, the ever-changing garden of colour below the water enchanted her, and Johnny grinned at her expressions of delight and wonder. "You'll get used to it all. A couple of weeks and you won't even notice it!"

"Never! I could never get used to this. It's so beautiful!"

At last he reached towards the controls, the engine sprang to life and they glided towards the shore. When they reached the shallows instead of leaping from the boat, she came to his side. "You promised to teach me how to run her. Remember?"

"Sure. Nothing to it. Look, I'll show you —"

Seated at the controls she quickly mastered the rudiments of starting the engine and steering the craft. When at length Johnny tossed the anchor up on to the sand and they began to wade ashore she congratulated herself on having at least picked up a few points on how to manage the old *Katrina*. Tomorrow she could take the boat out for a short spin by herself, Johnny had told her. She could hardly wait for the time to come! They were strolling together over the sand when he paused, looking towards the house. "Damn!"

"What's the matter?" Puzzled by his tense and angry expression, she followed his gaze towards the curving road. A long red car was slowing to a stop at the entrance to the guest house.

"Not to worry," she chided him lightly, "could be it's a new guest for the Islander –"

"It is," he replied woodenly. "He's turned up a day early. It's him – Kinnear." He swung around on a bare heel. "I'm off –"

"But you can't –" she began.

"Can't I? You just watch me! You can pass on the message that I'm otherwise engaged. I am too." He threw her a triumphant grin as a mini-bus appeared around the palm-fringed point of the beach. "Well, this lets me out –"

"But won't he want to see you, about the alterations ... and everything?"

Tight-lipped, he flung over his shoulder, "He doesn't need any advice from *me* about the Islander. Seeing he's got all these ideas about doing up the old shack, let him get on with it!"

In silence she watched him stride away.

CHAPTER III

SHE too would have been happy to escape a meeting with David Kinnear, Robyn thought, as with dragging footsteps she made her way over the expanse of creamy sand. Already, however, the long red car had turned in at the entrance to the guesthouse and she had an uneasy suspicion that he might already have caught sight of her.

All she could do now was to put off the ordeal for as long as possible, and if only she could gain the shelter of her bure while he was still in the main building ... Skirting the entrance she slipped over the grass between the thickly growing palm trees and soon she was letting herself into the thatched hut. Inside the small dwelling she ran a comb through salt-encrusted hair and added a touch of pink to her lips. At length, when she knew that to delay further would merely serve to give him all manner of mistaken ideas, like thinking that she was deliberately avoiding him (well, wasn't she?), she closed the door behind her. What was it he had told her on taking leave of her at Nandi? "*If* you're still interested by then." Well, she knew the answer to that one! She wasn't, not in him, not any longer!

Her reluctant steps brought her along the path leading to the house and she came upon him unexpectedly. Kneeling on the long grass, he was extending a tape along an outside wall. At the sight of her he straightened. "Hello, Robyn!" His smile was as heart-catching as ever, but she was aware of a shade of watchfulness in the dark eyes. "Just thought I'd take these measurements," he said easily. "Make a ground plan for a start and work from there."

Just as though the whole matter had already been discussed between them, she thought indignantly. Was he mocking her? The part-owner who wasn't even a "part"; who was in no position to confer in the updating of the old place. She stole

48

a quick glance towards him, but he appeared to be perfectly serious.

Taking a small pad from the breast pocket of his cotton shirt, he noted down a figure with his ball-point. "Johnny around?"

"No," she said stiffly. "He's down on the beach with the coral boat, taking some guests from the hotel out to the reef." Glad of an excuse to get away, she offered hopefully, "I can go and catch him before he leaves if you like?" Or try to, she amended silently.

"It doesn't matter. I'll have a word with him when he gets back. You don't mind if I carry on with this?"

"Go right ahead," she muttered, adding ungraciously, "It's all yours anyway!"

He didn't appear to have caught the low words. "What I had in mind," he was saying pleasantly, "was to alter the whole place into small apartment blocks, make each one into a self-contained unit with every convenience I can think up. Air-conditioning, that's a must in this climate, rubber mattresses on the beds, electric stoves, decently appointed bathrooms with showers, refrigerators. After that what the show will need will be a first-class restaurant. There'll be some guests who prefer to eat out all the time and others who may prefer to do for themselves through the day and have a slap-up evening meal. It's got to be really something that dining room with a first-class chef." He smiled down at her. "All this with your approval, of course."

"What difference does it make what *I* think?" There, she had come right out with it. He could no longer pretend to ignore her feelings in the matter.

Maddeningly he chose to disregard her resentful words. "This is just the beginning." His attitude had the effect of making her young and foolish when actually *he* was the one who should be feeling embarrassed at the situation. Reluctantly she brought her mind back to the deep vibrant tones. "There'll be a swimming pool, of course. Luckily there's room to put one down in front of the main building without interfering with the natural look of the place." He swung around towards the palm-covered slopes fronting the ocean. "I thought, to tie in with the general environment, bures scattered here and there around the grounds amongst the coconut palms, not in a row like they are now. These'll be small huts with thatched roofs, woven walls, but once you're inside, real down-to-earth comfort and coolness to suit the climate. Fiji is one of the few places in the world where the past still lives on unspoiled. What I'm aiming for is a sort of primitive Fijian art effect all tied up with modern luxury. If there's anything else you can dream up to add to the general picture?"

The small devil of resentment that was driving her made her say waspishly, "Who cares?"

"Not you, apparently."

"Why should I? It's your idea, your plans, it's nothing to do with me!"

"Except that you happen to be a part owner –"

That really made her blaze. "So *you* say! But that's not what it's like really ... not now ... since you came and took over."

His mouth tightened. "It seems there's no pleasing you. If your idea is to make me mad you're doing fine."

She was aware of her heightened colour. "Good! Now you'll know how it feels."

At last she had sparked an answering flash of anger in the dark eyes. He turned away, running the extension tape beneath and noting a figure on the pad. "You are a funny girl. You don't seem to want me to help you and your brother out of the mess you've got yourselves into."

"Leave Johnny out of it." Her voice was muffled.

"I only wish I could. Hmm, that's a wide room ... have to allow for it in the alterations. Sorry," he glanced towards her politely, "you were saying –"

"Oh, you know what I mean," she burst out with feeling. "Buying the schooner was something he did as he thought for the best. It was a good idea really. He'd have made a lot of money out of it – maybe even enough to renovate the Islander, if things had turned out as he planned. How was he to know that there'd be an accident and the ship would get holed on a coral reef on her first trip out?"

"Accidents, as you term it, aren't unknown around these island waters," he said with a cold anger that made her wonder with a prick of alarm if perhaps she had gone too far. "That's why owners of yachts and schooners, especially valuable ones, usually make a point of taking out a decent amount of insurance to cover any eventualities."

"There was insurance," she flashed.

He slanted her a glance, then returned to his task. "That's right," he conceded briefly. "Some."

"Anyway," driven by an impulse she didn't pause to define, she followed him around a corner of the house and stood watching as he noted figures in his wretched little pad, "he's going to do all he can to help to get things going again, with the guesthouse, I mean."

"Good. Did he tell you?"

"Yes, no – well, I just know he is. He's that sort of person."

"Look here, Robyn," he turned to face her and at the expression in the calm brown eyes she dropped her gaze, a trifle ashamed of the way she was treating him. "Tell me, just how well do you know Johnny?"

"He's my brother! We were kids together! He'd never do anything mean or underhand. He just ... gets carried away sometimes. He believes what other people tell him. You could say he was a bit too optimistic, but only just sometimes," she added hastily. "Oh, I know he's not being very co-operative right now, but you can't blame him for feeling the way he does. Once he gets over the shock of it all and cools down a bit, I'm sure he'll feel differently."

"I see."

What did he see? she thought in panic. That she was protesting too much, too quickly? That all she had told him about Johnny could be merely her own loyal imagination? But it was all true, she knew it was. One only had to look at him.

"You believe me, don't you?" she said uncertainly.

He didn't answer but went on measuring just as though he hadn't heard her. Perhaps, she thought hopefully, he hadn't.

"I'll go and tell him you're here," she offered, and made her escape.

The awful shame-making part of it all was that in spite of everything she still liked him. She couldn't help herself. What she really meant was, she corrected her whirling thoughts, was that she would have liked him quite a lot, had things been different. As it was ... she put aside the traitorous thoughts and moved down to the beach where Johnny was helping a party of tourists out of the motor boat. She waded through the shallow water until she reached him.

"Kinnear still there?" he asked.

"Yes," she whispered, "he's taking measurements of the outside walls. Says he's making a ground plan of the place and he's going to work from that."

"Well, if he's there for the day I'm not hanging around. He gets under my skin! Tell him I won't be back for a while." The next moment the engine sprang into life and the boat was spinning over the placid water, a white spindrift spraying from the bow.

Lucky Johnny, to escape so easily! The group who had been taken to the reef in the coral boat were getting into a mini-bus that would transport them back to their hotel around the point. Robyn passed them and went on towards the house. With a sense of relief she saw that David Kinnear was no longer on the path, then rounding a bend, she came face to face with him. "Oh," the words came in a flurry, "Johnny said to tell you he's sorry but he can't get back just now. He'll fix things up with you later."

He nodded, showing no sign of surprise, and she wondered if he believed her. She'd always been hopelessly inadequate when it came to successfully putting over lies and evasions.

She went on to the bure and, conscious of an odd restlessness, picked up a sketch pad and began to work furiously. Before long the outlined design of a stylized picture of native

52

flowers and palms and sea-shells appeared on the sketch pad, and soon she was taking out brushes and paints. One of the advantages of an absorbing hobby, the thought intruded itself, was that it kept you from dwelling too much on a certain brown-eyed man a few yards distant; stopped you from wanting to return and do battle with him once again. She worked on until a light knock arrested her and wiping paint-smeared hands on her smock, she opened the door to Pam.

"Am I disturbing you?"

"I'm due for a break." Robyn smiled into Pam's wistful face. "Take a seat on the bed."

"Do you do much art work?"

Robyn laughed. "I never get enough time at it. At least that's how it's always been up till now, but here everything's different. Someone else to cook the dinner, Selani and the girls to do the housework, and all I have to worry about is taking out the coral boat when the tide's right. It's the chance of a lifetime! And with this depth of colour in the atmosphere and all this fascinating Fijian primitive art —"

"I like it." The other girl had come to stand at her side, her absent gaze resting on the colourful mural with its brilliant shadings. "Don't be too sure you can work here at anything for long, though, not unless you can beat the enemy —"

"Enemy?"

"The laziness, the 'tomorrow will do' atmosphere of the islands. I suppose it's the humid heat or something, but it's awfully hard to fight against it. Not so bad for me, I'm only here for a day or two at a time in between flights." She lapsed into silence and seemed to be thinking of something else.

"Do you smoke?"

"Thanks." She took a cigarette from the packet Robyn was extending towards her. "I do, just sometimes, when I'm worried to death —"

"Worried?" Robyn held a lighter to the other girl's cigarette.

"Well, yes. Actually," she flicked an imaginary speck of

53

dust from her short shift, "it's just ... Johnny. You don't happen to know where he is?"

Robyn considered. "He was down at the beach taking some tourists from the hotel out to see the coral gardens, then afterwards he took off in the boat—"

"Did he say where he was going?" The brown eyes were wide and anxious.

"No, but I think he'll be away for the rest of the day."

"He doesn't want to see me, that's why he's taken off," Pam murmured in a low tense tone. "Oh, I feel such a fool, coming here, hoping we'll make things up. I hate myself for coming! Love! It makes you do these crazy things. You can't seem to help yourself."

Robyn was trying to understand the reason for the other girl's passionate outburst. At last she asked gently, "What was the trouble between you and Johnny? What happened?"

"That wretched schooner," Pam breathed on a deep sigh. "If only he hadn't got in with the wrong crowd and put money into it. I happen to know one or two of that group, and the money for the purchase of the boat was mostly Johnny's. When it came to the crunch the other two could barely rake up enough to make much difference. It was agreed that Johnny was to be skipper and he was all wrapped up in his plans. By the time he had the craft ready for sailing he'd spent so much on it that he didn't even have enough left to get a decent amount of insurance on it ... worse luck. Now," she ran on in a distressed tone, "Johnny's lost the lot. He told me that he's had to borrow from the architect here to get the place done up in the hope that it will start paying for itself and repay the loan. But all that will take ages and ages." With nervous fingers she plucked at a corner of the cotton bedspread. "I've known Johnny for six months now, ever since I got transferred to the New Zealand–Australia–Fiji run. We were going to be married one of these days, but now ... We were engaged, you see, then he broke everything off. 'Finish', he said."

"Is it because of the money he owes to David Kinnear?"

"Is it ever! He's got these quaint old-fashioned notions that unless a man has a rich wife he shouldn't get married until he can afford to support her. You know? Build a huge house, fill it with expensive furniture, all that nonsense. I think the idea of being so deeply in debt simply terrifies him and nothing I can say makes the slightest difference. He just can't see that we could get over the hurdle. I could help with the payments for the loan. It wouldn't be for ever. They tell me David Kinnear's a nice guy, he wouldn't be too hard. We could wipe off the debt, together. But no, Johnny's so stubborn. It's his pride that's at the bottom of it all. Actually," the red lips curved in a rueful smile, "we almost came to blows over it. We had a big row the last time I was here and it finished up with me hurling the ring back at him and vowing I'd never come to the Islander again." Her voice broke. "But then I thought, maybe by now he'll have had time to think things over and everything will be all right. But now," all at once her eyes were glittering with unshed tears, "I've got to report back at the airport at seven."

"He'll be back by then," Robyn assured her, but they both knew it was only a faint hope.

"I don't know why I'm worrying you with all this. Stupid, isn't it, caring so much, I mean. It's over, that's what he's trying to tell me, and if I had any pride, even a grain of it, I'd stop coming here on the chance." Pam raised troubled eyes. "I just can't believe he's stopped caring." She stubbed out her cigarette in a fan shell lying on the low table, "if only he doesn't go back to *her*!" she finished.

"Who do you mean?"

"Oh, just a girl he used to be friendly with before he met me. Noeline's always around, hoping he'll come back to her. Anyone can see it. She's got oodles of cash, her father's one of the wealthiest business men in Fiji, right at the top in travel promotion. I'm so afraid Johnny will —" She broke off with a tremulous smile. "You must think I'm awful, running on like this. I'm not usually such a misery —"

"But if he was planning to marry you," Robyn said cheerfully, "he couldn't have thought all that much of her. I don't see what you're worrying about."

"It's just," Pam's voice was choked with emotion, "that she cared for him ... she still does. She hates me for what she regards as stealing him from her. She's spoiled and arrogant and – Oh, I don't know why I'm saying these horrible things! It's just his being so beastly to me, ignoring me, acting as though I wasn't here. He must know I've come just to see him." Her mouth quivered. "What's nearly driving me crazy is the thought that he's away in Suva – with her. Why can't I forget Johnny?" she cried passionately. "He's nothing outstanding, got lots of faults. He's far too easy-going and gets talked into things, like paying out the biggest share of the money for the boat. He's far too optimistic too – always planning some grand money-making scheme that somehow never eventuates. But that wouldn't be so bad if he didn't have these stupid ideas, I suppose you could call it chivalry. I call it being stubborn. He's just about the stubbornest man I've ever known ... wouldn't you agree? It's that stupid pride of his, it ruins everything," she ran on without waiting for an answer. "When he's on top, there's no one like Johnny, but he just can't bear to take second place. Know what I mean?"

"Don't ask me," sighed Robyn.

"Oh, I forgot. You two are almost strangers, aren't you! Well, let me tell you that once he gets an idea into his head you may as well say good-bye to ever changing it. Heaven knows why I love him," she murmured moodily, "I just ... do." With a deep sigh she rose to her feet. "But if he thinks I'm going to wait around here for him for ever –"

There was nothing Robyn could find to say.

"I'm off down the beach for a swim," Pam said listlessly from the doorway. "It's something to do. Coming?"

"Okay. Meet you down there in a few minutes."

Swiftly Robyn changed from her shift into a gay pink swim-suit and soon she and Pam were crossing the sand, running together towards the waters of the warm blue Pacific. All at once she caught sight of David. He was moving around a corner of the house and with swift strokes she began to swim away. She didn't want him to think she was hoping he would come down to join them. She floated lazily on the shimmering sea, lulled into a sense of dreamy relaxation by the sound of the surf breaking over the reef and the warmth of sun and sea. How happy she had been that day ... and he'd seemed to like her too ... a little. Perhaps if everything had been different, if it hadn't been for Johnny ... Dreams, idle thinking. Everything was different, and she had promised Johnny she would be on her guard against David Kinnear. Not, she thought wryly as she swam to join the dark cap visible in the water ahead of her, that there seemed much need to watch herself in that direction. The David of today was apparently interested in nothing but his work at the old guesthouse. Their memorable day together at Castaway Island might never have been.

At last she and Pam splashed their way from the shallows, to drop down on the sand, faces upturned to the sun. When they returned to the house Robyn could see no sign of David. Pam said she would take a nap and Robyn decided to return to her painting. She enjoyed working with acrylic paints and the mural was shaping well. Indeed, it gave promise of being the best thing she had done, perhaps because she herself was so enchanted with the wealth of tropical flowers and greenery.

When she entered the bure her swimsuit had dried, and without troubling to change, she picked up brushes and paints and went on with her task. So absorbed was she in her work that when at last she finished the picture, a glance at the small travelling clock on the bureau told her that three hours had flown by. She wondered if David had gone from the house yet, but peering from the window, she caught a gleam of a red car amidst a screen of palm trees. Robyn didn't know whether she was relieved or dismayed to find he was still here.

When she had showered she dressed in the minimum of garments needed in the hot climate – brief underclothing, an orange-coloured shift, the woven straw scuffs she had pur-

57

chased at the hotel shop in Nandi – she combed out the long hair, still slightly damp after her swim. Then, picking up the mural together with a handful of drawing pins, she went along the passage to the big living room. She couldn't wait to see how the picture would look when it was up on the wall.

No one was about at the moment and when she had pinned the mural above the mantel she stood back critically. There were faults, of course. Somehow no art work ever succeeded in matching up to the preconceived picture you had in mind when you began, but there was no doubt it livened up the room. The colours, subdued yet brilliant, appeared to glow in the fading light.

She was in the hallway, hoping to come across Mrs. Daley and tell her what she had done, when a masculine figure arose from where he had been bending over the skirting boards.

"Oh, hello," Robyn said lamely, "still at it?"

"Nearly finished. Now I can go right ahead and get on with drawing up the plans. Might want a bit of help from you, once I get started. Just a line on how you'd like things done, especially when it comes to the decorating. Ideas of colour and decor, you know?"

"Oh yes, I –" She checked herself, recollecting in the nick of time who he was and who she was. She curbed her natural enthusiasm and said stiffly, "It's up to you to do what you wish with the place."

"Just the same, I'd be grateful for some ideas. Planning of the flower gardens, what to plant around the pool, a colour scheme for the restaurant, all that."

"Go right ahead and do what you like," she said in a tight voice. "You will anyway, won't you? Wasn't that in the agreement?"

Still he refused to be drawn. He merely grinned that lazy grin, said gently, "Agreements can be bent around to suit sometimes, you'd be surprised how easy it is! Not to worry, maybe you'll change your mind later when you get more idea of how the place will look when it's finished."

"Maybe I won't!" If he heard the low words he made no

58

sign but continued to glance around the room in an assessing businesslike manner. "It'll work out quite well changing the place into apartments; not too costly an alteration. I thought we'd have the restaurant a little distance away from the main building, connect it with a thatched roof over a passageway in between, to carry out the island decor."

Robyn was silent. Apparently however her obvious lack of enthusiasm for his projects didn't affect him in the least. He was regarding her with the amused tolerance that was somehow so much more maddening than straight-out anger. "I think we can do a good job –"

"We?"

"That's right. I'm counting on you to give me a hand with the details."

"But I told you, it has nothing to do with me."

He ignored that. His gaze was fixed on a painting hanging above her head, a picture done in oils and depicting a vividly-coloured sunset scene. "That sort of thing is out – definitely! Pictures of that type do nothing for a place. Over-coloured, unreal, they're not even good paintings! They seem to be dotted all over the house. The artist, whoever he was, must have stayed here for quite a while."

"He did," Robyn replied frigidly. "He was my father and he owned the Islander."

Now that at last she had cracked his cool composure she was too upset to notice. "And they're not all that bad. Johnny says there really are sunsets like that here in Fiji."

"Johnny said?" There it was again, the ever so slight but unmistakable note of contempt in his tone.

"Yes, Johnny," she flashed. "Oh, I know he's not an artist, but he knows."

To her surprise his voice was gentle. "Of course if you really want the pictures kept we'll find places for them, even if they're not to everyone's taste."

"It doesn't matter," she muttered.

It seemed, however, that there was no putting him out of his easy stride. He was gathering up pen and notebook, slipping the extension tape into the pocket of his shirt. "Well, I guess that about wraps it up for today, except for one thing –"

"What was that?"

Unconsciously she tensed herself for a cutting reply.

"Oh, just that I thought it was about time you saw a bit of Fijian native customs. They put on an Island dinner once a month at the big hotel just around the point from here. I thought you might like to come along and sample some native foods, see a few Fijian dancers. It's quite a night, especially if you've never seen anything like it before. Have you?"

"No, but –"

"Great! They start about seven and to get into the spirit of it all you're supposed to dress up in a sulu or a sarong, but don't worry if you haven't a sulu –"

"I have. It's not that. It's just –"

"Well then ... what are we waiting for?" The brown eyes were warm and friendly. All at once she was finding it very difficult to refuse the invitation, but of course she must. What would Johnny say if he came back tonight to find her in league with the enemy?

"Sorry, but I just can't make it."

He studied her for a moment and she dropped her gaze, horrified to feel the pink colour creeping up her cheeks. But it took more than a mere dinner invitation refusal to put Mr. David Kinnear out, it seemed. His smile was as relaxed as ever. "Too bad you can't make it ... but there'll be another time."

Privately she thought this was being over-optimistic in the circumstances, but she didn't say so. She was flooded with an absurd feeling of disappointment. What fun it would have been, dancing under a star-pricked sky, having her first glimpse of primitive customs, trying out native food, *with David*. She couldn't understand herself, feeling like this.

"Another one next month," he was saying, and moved along the passage. When they reached the open doorway leading into the big dining room, he paused abruptly, gave a low whistle of appreciation. "Now why haven't I seen that before? That's really something!"

"What is?" She realised now that he was staring up at the glowing mural pinned above the mantel.

"Now that's what I call a painting!" He moved into the room and regarded the picture closely. "Just the sort of thing I had in mind for the focal point in the new restaurant, something that would grab the attention as soon as you entered the room. What a stroke of luck, coming across someone who can do work of that calibre. Not that there aren't swags of artists around the place, the Pacific islands are full of them, but this particular one happens to have a certain gift. He's managed to pin down the atmosphere of the islands in colour ... difficult to explain ... but I like it. I like it very much! I'll find the artist and commission him to do some work for me." He stepped closer, examining the picture. "Can't see any signature."

"Don't bother looking." It was hard to keep the note of triumph subdued in her voice. "I did it. Finished it this afternoon, so if you don't mind, don't touch it. The paints aren't quite dry."

"*You!*" An expression of incredulous delight spread over his face. "Of all the luck! But, Robyn, that's fantastic! You've got yourself a job, did you know, designing the murals for the new Pacific Islander Motel?" She couldn't help a surge of pleasure. He looked as delighted as though he'd found the most talented artist in the islands, instead of just someone who happened to have hit on a media he was looking for.

He was eyeing her attentively. "You wouldn't have any objection to a commission for paintings, would you?"

She forgot all about being crushing and dignified and instead cried: "Oh no, I'd love to do them!"

"Right! That's settled, then. How about a long mural, twice the length of this one, suitable for hanging in a foyer? If you could work in something featuring primitive native art, with a predominating motif of the sea ... coral, tropical fish, shells, maybe a tortoise, it's an emblem of the islands. You'll know what to do."

Her eyes were alight with pleasure. "I'll give it a go."

"That's my girl! I've got to get along. Tell your brother I'll be back some time during the week with the plans. Then you can both have a look over them and see what you think of the layout. 'Bye!"

She watched him go with a wild impulse to call him back, tell him she had changed her mind about his invitation to the island feast. She couldn't understand herself. It wasn't as though she liked him *that way*. The surge of regret that had swept over must have been because of missing a novel experience, especially as the "*makiti*" would have given her valuable material for the murals he had commissioned her to paint.

Restlessly she made her way to the kitchen, where smiling Fijian men were tossing green salads and transferring them into big wooden bowls in preparation of the evening meal.

Mrs. Daley strolled across the spacious, immaculate room towards her. "I saw you go down to the beach. That's the first thing my daughter does when she comes here to see me –"

"Oh, you have a family? Johnny didn't say –"

Mrs. Daley laughed merrily. "My goodness, yes. Two boys and two girls. The girls are married now, one of them lives over in Sydney and the two younger boys are still at University ... they live together in the house at Suva. Did you enjoy your swim?"

"Oh yes, it was super. Pam came down with me."

"Not Johnny?"

"No."

"Poor Pam." A shadow passed over Mrs. Daley's sun-tanned features. "I don't know what's gone wrong between those two, but it's such a pity. They suit each other so well. They were getting married in a couple of months. Funny, isn't it, how things can change all of a sudden. Pam's taking it hard. I only hope he doesn't go back to *her*."

Robyn didn't wish to appear inquisitive, but her feelings were getting the better of her. "You mean Noeline?"

The older woman nodded. "He was well out of that," she

said succinctly. "Pam's a darling. He's a fool if he throws away a chance of marrying a girl like that. She's crazy about him too, anyone can see it." She turned aside at the approach of a Fijian house-girl.

It must be dreadful, Robyn mused, to love someone so much that nothing else mattered, not even pride. A lovely girl like Pam, smart, poised, attractive, who could surely choose from any number of attractive young men, yet here she was hopelessly, desperately in love with Johnny. Robyn found herself hoping that she never fell in love to that extent, and for no reason at all a face flashed across her mental vision. David Kinnear, with his affable, tantalising smile.

She thrust the picture away and wrenched her mind back to Mrs. Daley's tones. "Noeline's got wealthy parents and they've absolutely spoiled her from the time she was born. What could you expect with four brothers coming along first? She's as hard as can be and she'll get her own way at whatever cost to anyone else. It was just lucky that Johnny found out his mistake in time and called the wedding off, even if it was at the very last moment ... three days before the ceremony, actually. A girl like Noeline wouldn't forgive that in a hurry, I can tell you – Oh dear, you must think I'm awful, gossiping like this, but Johnny's like a son to me and in these small places you can't help knowing what's going on."

"Still ... three days before the wedding ... did she care?"

"Oh, she cared right enough! She was furious, but I can't imagine her feelings being hurt, more likely it was her pride."

"It wouldn't be very pleasant, being stood up at the last minute. Whatever was Johnny thinking of to let things go so far –"

The older woman's smile was quizzical. "He'd met Pam by then. I can't say that I blame him for what he did. Oh well, better late than never. You should thank fate that he met Pam in the meantime ... and keep your fingers crossed he doesn't change his mind again."

"It seems to me he's too popular with the women, that's Johnny's trouble."

Mrs. Daley said teasingly, "Including his sister?"

Robyn laughed, "I guess you could count me in too."

As she moved away she mused on the muddle of Johnny's affairs. She could only hope he would sort it out, *instead of running away*. The thought came out of the air and she thrust it aside. Come to that, she had problems of her own, one in particular with smiling dark eyes and an unflappable manner. She wished David Kinnear wouldn't persist in regarding her as a sort of overgrown schoolgirl. It wasn't as though he was all that old. Thirty was really a perfect age for a man. Heavens, where were her thoughts leading her? She wrenched her imaginings away and went out to the thatched-roofed patio where guests were lounging in bamboo chairs as they watched the approach of a fishing boat returning from a day's excursion to one of the outlying islands.

At that moment a yellow and black rental car braked to a stop on the path and a few moments later a group of air crew and hostesses passed her on their way inside. A little later they returned, accompanied by Pam. "This is Robyn!" the other girl told her companions, and immediately Robyn found herself drawn into the laughing, friendly group.

"We've got a reprieve," a young pilot was saying gaily. "The message has just come through that the plane's developed slight engine trouble of some sort and we're off duty until midnight!"

As the party settled themselves at a low table a young Fijian waiter, evidently accustomed to the air crew, welcomed each one by name. Soon he returned from the bar carrying a tray of long iced drinks which he put down on the low table.

"We're all going over to the island dinner at the Pacific," Pam said gaily.

Under cover of the babel of talk, Robyn whispered, "But what if Johnny should come back?"

Pam put down her glass. "I don't care any more." Robyn saw that the other girl was very pale, her eyes dark with despair. "I've been waiting here for hours, and what does *he* do? He takes off just to avoid seeing me. It's too bad he had to go to the trouble of spelling it out, but he won't need to any more. I'm finished with waiting around just like he's finished," all at once her voice broke, "with me."

Presently someone suggested a swim and a blond flight-engineer who was seated opposite fixed Robyn with his blue gaze. "Coming down for a dip? It cools you down, makes you fresh enough to get up the energy for the hotel dinner –"

"But I'm not –"

"You are, you know! It's all organised. Swim first, then the *makiti*."

Everyone dispersed to change into swimming trunks and bikinis and soon the party of men and girls were strolling towards the tide lapping softly on the sand below. Robyn was surprised to find the others so sun-tanned, but of course to the air crew on the jet-run between North America and Australia, swimming in the warm blue Pacific waters must provide a welcome change.

They stayed in the sea a long time. Robyn still couldn't become accustomed to not feeling chilly after being so long in the water.

When at last they made their way back along the sand, the sun was sinking over the sea in a spectacular blaze of apricot and gold.

It was later as they climbed into the station wagon that Robyn noticed Pam's swift searching glance along the darkening road, caught the other girl's disappointed sigh. The next moment Pam was gay again, laughing and chatting vivaciously as she squeezed into a seat between Robyn and a young co-pilot.

The road followed the curve of the bay and Robyn was surprised to find how near was the newly built modern hotel around the point from the Islander.

As they swept towards the big white building with its blaze of lights a red-haired air hostess leaned forward to touch the driver on the shoulder. "Don't forget that tonight it's sarongs for the girls, sulus for you men!"

Soon everyone was crowding into a small gift shop in the

65

foyer of the hotel. The group made their way towards the glorious array of softly flowing silks and vividly patterned cotton sulus heaped on the counters.

Robyn watched Pam choose a length of scarlet silk from the pile. Draping the material around her shoulders, she turned towards Robyn. "Now it's your turn."

"But I haven't an idea what to do with it."

"We'll show you."

With a wide and friendly smile a Fijian girl held towards Robyn a length of palest green silk embroidered in gold threads. Obligingly Robyn took it from the attendant. "Though I haven't a clue –"

"Allow me." Bruce, the blond flight-engineer, already wearing his skirt-like sulu, was at her side. In a few deft movements he had draped the flowing material around her. "Now, shut your eyes –" His laughing face was very close as, hands pinning her shoulders, he guided her towards the mirror. "Now you can look!"

Her face, flushed from the hours spent on the beach this afternoon, stared back at her.

"One more thing –" Taking from the native girl a fragrant, sweetly-perfumed lei of frangipani blossoms, he slipped the ring of flowers over her head.

Bruce was eyeing her with beaming approval and she had to admit that the delicate colouring of the silk sarong flattered her, lent her an air of deceptive fragility. Would David approve of her could he see her like this? If only she could stop herself from thinking of him!

CHAPTER IV

THE gentle strumming of native guitars fell around them as they left the car at the modern building facing the lagoon and made their way along a path lighted by flares in iron stanchions. The swift tropical night had fallen and fairy lights strung in the sweet-scented foliage overhead threw their gleam over smoke rising from a barbecue, the flower-bedecked islanders moving amongst long tables set on the grass.

Robyn took her seat with the others at a long table covered in banana leaves and tropical blooms and set with succulent sea-foods and native delicacies. There were lobsters, prawns, mounds of fresh fruit, pineapple, paw-paw, golden melons – jugs of coconut milk.

Bruce, the flight-engineer, followed her gaze towards a heaped wooden platter. "That's *kokoda*."

"Sorry," Robyn said with a smile, "but I still don't know –"

"To you," he interpreted, "raw fish marinated in coconut cream. And don't be put off by the 'raw' part. It's delicious. Let me help you to some –"

"Wait a minute," Pam called gaily. "First she has to have a drink – Talei."

Robyn glanced down at the glass with an orchid clinging to the rim, that the waiter had set down before her.

Laughingly Bruce raised his glass. "It's almost Fiji's national cocktail. I'll even give you the recipe if you like! You take some Bacardi –"

"Add a dash of rum, passion-fruit nectar and bitter lemon," a co-pilot put in. "Serve decorated with a frangipani flower –"

"And don't forget a sliver of sugar-cane for a swizzle-stick," Pam cried laughingly. "Afterwards you can chew the stick – like this!"

Pam was strung-up, excited, talkative, a different person entirely, Robyn thought, from the distraught heartbroken girl of earlier in the day. If Pam was wearing a mask she wore it well and no one would guess that her gaiety wasn't of the genuine variety.

Soon, to the infectious beat of guitars throbbing through the darkness, Fijian girls and men approached the coconut mat outspread on the grass for entertainers. Robyn watched as fibre skirts and flower leis swung as the troupe swayed in the graceful rhythm of their native dances.

Presently their place was taken by a Fijian girl, young and attractive with her flowing, flower-bedecked hair and long sulu skirt. In the still air her voice rose poignantly sweet in the age-old melodies of the Pacific islands.

She was followed by a stamping band of warriors, upraised pointed spears in their hands, shark-tooth ornaments in their ears. The wild movements and ferocious cries left no doubt as to the significance of the war dance.

It was all novel and colourful. Robyn, applauding with the others, wondered why she wasn't enjoying the entertainment more, instead of feeling merely as though she were watching a scene in a play. Come on now, admit it. If only David Kinnear had brought her here everything would have been excitingly different. Wasn't that the reason too why she found herself glancing around her in search of a certain dark masculine head? It was a long drive back to Suva. He might be staying at this hotel for the night. Not that she wanted to see him here, not after having refused his invitation. She was just . . . wondering . . . But in the warm velvety darkness she could see little beyond the flare-lighted radius of the tables. And anyway, she chided herself, in this gay company why on earth was she wasting time thinking of anyone else, especially *him!*

The dinner was coming to an end now and couples were leaving the tables to move over the grass and join the guests who danced under a canopy of stars.

"Dance, Robyn?" A trembling ran along her nerves. Wouldn't you just know that David would appear tonight, after she'd refused his invitation to join him at the island dinner? Giving her no time for explanations, he drew her

68

to her feet and in a few moments they were moving to the pulsing beat of singing guitars.

In the glimmer of the fairy-lights overhead, she searched his face. He appeared as affable, as cool as ever. What had she expected? Disappointment at finding her here with a party after having refused his own invitation? Annoyance? But of course it would take a lot more than that to shake his cool composure. Don't forget, she chided herself, that he regards you as a silly schoolgirl, an unknown girl whose company he's forced to endure because of a business deal.

"I changed my mind," she told him breathlessly, moving to the tempo of an island melody, "about coming here tonight, I mean."

He merely nodded smilingly, *uncaringly*. Clearly what she did was a matter of indifference to him. She wasn't important enough in his scheme of things for it to make any difference, one way or the other. The thought was somehow unbearable. Suddenly it became very necessary to make him understand. Unconsciously her movements slowed to a routine in time with the beat. "I didn't mean to go to the dinner when I was talking to you, then afterwards Pam wanted to come and all of a sudden I –"

"Had second thoughts. I'm glad you did."

Somehow the cheerful words were more hurtful than straight-out annoyance. They made her feel more than ever stupidly young, and awkward, and foolish. "Are you – staying here?"

"Just for the night. Actually I was hoping to run across someone here, someone I knew."

"Oh! Did he – she turn up?"

"Yes, wasn't I lucky!"

The notes of music died away and David strolled across the grass beside her. At the table he left her and her swift sideways glance showed her he was moving to join a group seated a short distance away. She strained her eyes in an effort to distinguish the woman seated beside him, but the crowd obscured her vision.

Around her the light chatter became general, until a smiling young Fijian waiter approached them, saying in his soft tones: "Airport control is on the phone with a message for the captain. Could you speak to them, please?"

"I'll be right there." The captain left the table, to return in a few minutes, a wry grin curving his lips.

"Don't tell me," called the red-haired air hostess, "let me guess! You've gotta go fly your plane –"

"Right! They managed to fit in the new engine sooner than they expected and we're due back at the airport right away. We can just make it if we step on the gas!"

"Who'd be an air hostess?" Pam joined the others standing in a group around the table. As goodbyes were called, she turned back towards Robyn. "Sorry we can't take you home! But you'll be all right," she added carelessly. "You can get David Kinnear to take you back to the Islander."

"Don't worry about me. 'Bye!'"

She watched the group as they moved into the darkness pricked by flickering flares. Get David Kinnear to take you! That would be the last thing she'd do! She had other ideas on the subject. Feeling all at once conspicuously alone at the deserted, leaf-covered table, she slipped unnoticed into the shadows, found a winding path beneath the trees and soon she was down on the starlit sands below.

There was no moon, but the southern sky blazed with stars and the murmur of the surf breaking on the reef drowned out the haunting notes of the island band. Drowned too the sound of footsteps. When a vibrant *familiar* voice behind her called, "Hi, Robyn, wait for me!" she froze.

In a moment he had caught up with her. "You didn't think you'd get away that easily, did you?" he laughed, and linked her fingers in his.

She was swept by a heady excitement. It was because of him that her feelings were so mixed up. She should hate him. In a way she did – but in another way ... And how could you think straight about anything when he was clasping her hand in his, drawing her closer, saying in that relaxed way

70

of his, "That's the trouble with you, little one. You're always running away —"

"I'd be all right on my own —"

"Better this way."

She was waging a losing battle against her own senses, and the languid tropical night. The gentle wash of waves on the beach, palms outlined against a dark sky, it wasn't fair. But she made an effort to pull her thoughts together. "How about your ... friend? Won't she ... miss you?" Horrified, she caught the betraying note of feeling in her tones.

"It was you," he said calmly, and tightened his arm around her.

"Well!" She turned to face him, but at something in his expression the words died away. All at once her heart was beating thud, thud, thud and a delicious warmth was stealing through her senses. "But I told you I wasn't coming. I ... didn't know myself."

"But you wanted to come — admit it, Robyn!" The teasing tones softened, deepened. "It was just that you didn't want *me* to bring you along. That was it, wasn't it?"

She didn't know how to reply, so correctly had he divined her state of mind, and she'd thought she'd been so convincing. It would be easy to fall in with his mood. Easy, and disastrous, for whatever would Johnny say if he returned to find her fraternising with the enemy? His enemy and hers ... or was that really the truth? Confused by the caressing note in his voice, his touch, she said very low, "Being under an obligation to someone makes a difference, and with Johnny feeling about you the way he does —"

"Robyn! Look at me!" But she knew that to do that would be to lose her argument and wrenching her hand free of his clasp, she hurried on.

"You're in a big hurry," he observed, "for a stroll along the beach. Hasn't anyone ever told you that no one ever hurries in Fiji?" Suddenly he had dropped down and pulled her down beside him on the sand. "Mmmm ... heady stuff, frangipani. I wanted to have a word with you —"

71

All at once the magic slipped away. He was the man Johnny hated, the man he had warned her about, and they both entirely in his power.

"It wasn't Johnny's fault, what happened," she said with spirit, "he did *try*! What's wrong with enjoying yourself, anyway?"

"Nothing. I'm all for it, so long as —"

"I know what you're going to say — so long as it isn't on someone one else's money!" Why couldn't he understand that Johnny was particularly vulnerable because of hurt pride, that later when he'd had time to get over the loss of the schooner, he would feel differently about everything? "Well, it wasn't like that with me. Coming here, I mean. If I'd known about Johnny —"

"Couldn't we leave your brother out of it, just for tonight?"

"It was you," she said in a low tone, "who wanted to have a word about all that."

"About you and me, Robyn! Just the two of us! No Johnny, no debts, nothing like that. Let's take it from here, shall we? It's start-again time, didn't you know?"

"It's not as simple as all that," she pointed out in a distressed tone. "Johnny thinks you —"

"I get it. Brother John blames me for the lot. But do you have to be all on his side? If he behaves himself —"

"There you go," she flashed, "expecting him to do what *you* want him to! That's what he hates. He thinks you want him here for your runabout man."

For a moment he was silent. "Does it ever occur to you or your brother," came the lazy tones, "that what I'm doing is for your benefit too? I'm on your side, Robyn. Think of the profits that are going to come rolling in once we get the place known about."

"Profits for you!"

"And you."

"You're a funny girl." He raised a hand and very gentle brushed back the long hair blowing across her face in the night breeze.

Nervously she plucked at the creamy blossoms of the flower necklace. It was the silence that was dangerous. It did things to her, made her forget everything but his nearness.

His voice softened, deepened. "Do you have to try so hard, Robyn?"

"Try?"

"Hating me. It didn't seem to bother you out at Castaway the other day."

"Oh, but that was before – before . . ."

"I could change your mind, you know –"

At something in his tone she sprang to her feet. "Come on!" She had a traitorous suspicion that if she didn't leave him now, this minute, she'd be lost. She wouldn't want to leave him – ever. She made her way along the beach, her feet sinking into the soft sand at every step.

"It's no use running away –" She pretended not to hear him. "I can catch you up any time I want –" She felt herself stumble over a piece of driftwood lying in the shadows and the next moment, trembling, shaken, felt his arms around her. She wondered if he was going to kiss her and felt a betraying regret when he released her. They were approaching the Islander now and together took the winding track between the coconut palms that led towards her bure-style unit.

In the dark-blue, star-ridden night it took a lot of determination to force herself to turn away from him with a lightly spoken, "See you next time you're down here." He didn't even try to detain her, but as she took a step forward along the path he called softly, "Haven't you forgotten something?"

She swung around in surprise, realising too late his meaning as he caught her close. For a second she caught the glint in his eyes, then he bent his head low and everything merged into rapture. It was a kiss that stirred her, no use denying it, and she gave herself up to enchantment. Between them the perfume from the bruised blossoms rose heady and sweet. At length she drew herself free, heard his low laugh as she sped away. Quickly, quickly, Robyn, while you still retain a shred

73

of sanity! Up the shadowy path, into the bure, out of range of a magnetic attraction of a man who drew her against her will. She was still trembling as she lifted the flower lei from around her neck.

In the morning she was roused by a chorus of birdsong, throaty and sweet, from the palms high overhead. For a few moments she lay listening, wondering idly at her feeling of happiness left over from her dreams. Although why she should dream of David ... The frangipani lei lay on the table where she had flung it last night, the satiny petals fresh except where the petals had been crushed in his good-night embrace. Last night ...

Running water into the bath, she laid the flowers gently down, then went out into pearly freshness and colour and tropical growth.

When she reached the dining room Mrs. Daley greeted her with a smile.

"Morning. Is Johnny up yet?"

The older woman shook her head. "He took off last night and we expect him back always when we see him. Sometimes he doesn't show up for a day or two, other times it could be a week or a month. Usually he's away on some job or other, guiding a tourist party around the islands or helping to crew a boat."

He might have left a message for me, Robyn thought. Aloud she said, "But surely he must give you some idea of how long he'll be away —"

Mrs. Daley's indulgent smile did nothing to assuage Robyn's growing sense of apprehension. "Goodness, no! He likes to be free, to come and go as he pleases. He doesn't have to tell *me*, you know."

Robyn was puzzled. "But that means, then, that you have to carry on managing the place all the time he's gone?"

"My dear," there was a wry twist to the older woman's lips, "what difference does it make?"

"Well, it makes a difference to me," Robyn said with spirit.

"I think it's real mean of him! He could meet with an accident, anything could happen. He could at least send a note from wherever he is."

Mrs. Daley shrugged philosophical shoulders. "What would be the use? There'd be no address to send a reply to and by the time the letter arrived he'd most likely be back here anyway. He's probably a long way from mails where he is –"

"Yes, but –"

"Don't *worry*, dear, he'll turn up again. He always does."

Robyn stared back at her. "But what about the coral boat? What if someone from the hotel rings up and wants him to take a party out today?"

"They did, actually, just a few minutes ago. I said I'd ring them back in an hour. Not that I thought there'd be much chance of Johnny coming back by then – he usually takes off for a week or so at a time when he goes – but –"

"I'll take them out!"

Mrs. Daley's suntanned face expressed surprise. "You! But –" her expression cleared, "can you manage the boat?"

"Of course I can! Johnny showed me all about the controls the other day. Ring them back, Mrs. Daley. Tell them I'll meet them on the beach in an hour –"

The older woman hesitated. "Well, if you're quite sure you can cope –"

Robyn pushed aside any doubts she might have had on the matter. At the moment one thought only filled her mind and that was that she was determined to make an effort to repay at least something of the debt she and her brother owed to David Kinnear. And this was an easy way to do something about it. She would have preferred a little more practice with the old *Katrina*, but she had taken the boat out herself a short distance once or twice yesterday and on the calm waters of the lagoon she was sure she could manage it.

When she reached the beach a little later, the party was waiting for her, a group of tourists in holiday mood, glad of a diversion that would be a change in their pattern of sunbathing and swimming in the waters of the hotel pool. If only she were more informed on the nature of marine life! What if her passengers should enquire of her the scientific names of the brilliantly coloured shoals of fish, the mushroom-like growths, or waving seagrasses? She was fortunate, however, for the young crowd aboard were content to gaze down through the glass observation panels as with cries of "Oh!" and "Quick, look at that!" they took in the vibrant undersea gardens. The hour flew by, then she was guiding the *Katrina* back towards the shallows. Soon passengers, scuffs in their hands, were climbing over the side of the boat. They thanked her for the trip, then boarded the mini-bus that would take them around the sandy point and back to their hotel.

It was a pattern that repeated itself as the days went by. Robyn discovered on the shelf in the dining room a manual dealing with marine life in the warm reef waters and she now felt confident in being able to answer at least the usual queries made to her by passengers on the reef excursion.

Perhaps because sun and sea were having their way with her, as the days passed her concern for Johnny's safety lessened. It was evident that Eve Daley knew Johnny much better than she did ... his restlessness, his search for new sensations and above all, his hatred of being forced into a position of subservience to anyone. Hadn't Pam told her much the same thing? "He can't bear to take second place," she had said to Robyn. And the prospect of being David Kinnear's "runabout man" was just about the worst thing he could imagine! Another man might agree to put up with it for what it would mean to him in the future, but Johnny, never! He had to be first or not at all!

Each morning when she awoke she told herself hopefully, "Perhaps Johnny will come today." If only she could be as philosophical about his movements as Mrs. Daley, but then the older woman didn't have this feeling of doom. Of David Kinnear about to descend on her at any moment, a sheaf of papers tucked beneath his arm and a question in his eyes, asking in his deceptively quiet tones where Johnny was and when he would be back.

The only consolation of her brother's absence from the house was that her daily trips out to the reef had made her conversant with the gardens beneath the sea, and the big mural commissioned by David was at last completed. Perhaps because her imagination had been fired by the coral and sea-creatures, the picture done in acrylic paints approached more than anything she had yet done, her standard of perfection in her work. At any rate, it should please David and would constitute in a small way something towards paying off the insuperable mountain of debt that loomed between them.

At the end of the week there was still no word from Johnny. One afternoon she was returning after taking a party off tourists out to the reef in the *Katrina* when she glanced up to see David advancing towards her across the sand.

"Hey, I'll do that!" Hurrying to her side, he took the anchor and threw it up on the beach. His smiling glance ran over her, taking in the translucent apricot-tan of her skin. "Suits you –"

"What does?"

"The island tan."

"Oh, that . . ." Until this moment she had scarcely realised herself how different she must appear from the day of their first meeting. Now she was darkly tanned, bare-footed, her pink cotton shift bleached by the hot island sun.

"Your hair," he was saying appreciatively, "it's streaked with paler gold. To think that women go to hairdressers to get that effect and here you sit on the beach and collect it for free!"

She strolled beside him over the drifts of sand. "I don't just sit – at least, not all of the time!" Immediately the words were out she regretted them. How much did he know, she wondered, of Johnny's unexplained absence from the Islander? To change the subject she said quickly, "I suppose you've brought the plans for the alterations with you?"

"Uh-huh! I thought you and your brother could cast an eye over them, tell me what you think of the new image, be-

77

fore I draw up the final sketches. Is Johnny around today?"

"No." Frantically she wondered how long he had been at the house. Long enough for Mrs. Daley to have told him the truth? "Not today. He had to go away . . . on some business."

"Bad luck. Be away long, do you think?"

She hesitated. If she answered "yes", he would be suspicious of the true state of affairs. If she said "no", he would probably insist on waiting for Johnny's return. At last she murmured, "He didn't say." Adding, on an inspiration, "I know! You can leave the plans here with me and I'll show them to him later." She thrust aside a mental picture of Johnny's reaction to any suggestion of David's. "He'll get in touch with you afterwards. Yes, that would be the best way –"

"I've got a better idea –"

"You have?" She raised questioning eyes to his laughing glance.

"Sure! You'll do instead."

"Me! But I don't know the first thing about building. . . things like that. Anyway," in the nick of time she remembered who he was and how he figured in her scheme of things, "you'll know all about it. It's your business now."

"And yours. Come on, Rob, don't be like that!" He caught her hand in his, but she wrenched herself free. Why did this man's touch mean so much to her?

He didn't appear to notice, merely saying mildly, "I don't suppose you've made a start on the mural yet for the new restaurant?"

"As a matter of fact, I have. I've finished it!" *That* would surprise him, but of course he would never let it show.

"Pleased with it?"

For a moment she forgot who she was speaking to and conscious only of the interest in his face, spoke her thoughts aloud. "Oh, you know how it is with any art work, you never really feel satisfied with it. Somehow it never matches up with how you've imagined it at the beginning. But the subjects are pretty authentic. I had lots of chances to study all that underwater sea life going out in the *Katrina*."

"Good for you, Rob! I want to see that mural!"

When they reached the house there was no one on the shady verandah and he spread out on the old table a roll of plans he had taken from his pocket. "Run your eye over these, will you, Robyn?"

"I told you, it's no use asking me!" All at once it came to her that if she could give him her approval of the proposed alterations, and after all in view of his own financial involvement in the venture he would be sure to do the best for all concerned, then there would be no need for Johnny to go over the plans. She had a suspicion that the less her brother saw of David Kinnear the fewer stormy scenes there would be. "All right then, if you're happy about me looking them over instead of Johnny?"

"I'm happy! Look, Robyn, this is the new layout. It's only a rough draft, but you'll be able to get the general idea." As she bent over the neatly etched drawings she was surprised how easily she could follow the design of the buildings.

"No need to alter the outside walls of the place," David indicated the main building. "The old verandah will go, it's unsound anyway, and a wide patio can take its place, with trailing orchids at the end. Here's the swimming pool, in front of the main entrance. It will mean cutting down a few trees, but I'll keep that to a minimum. The way I look at it I don't want to move against the sculptural elements of the landscape but to go along with them. We'll have paths winding down amongst the coconut palms to the pool – what's on your mind?"

"Oh, it's just . . . I was thinking about the pool. There's an island out there somewhere," she waved a hand towards the shimmering expanse of sea, "where they tell me there are huge turtles. Do you know, they come when they're called by the natives of that particular island, they really do! I couldn't help thinking that a pool would be rather attractive if it was made in the shape of a big fat turtle."

"Good for you, Rob! You're a girl of ideas, as well as –" He broke off, glancing down at her bent head.

79

"As well as what?" she challenged him.

"Long term project," he said softly, "but I've got it all worked you ... tell you another time ... meantime, this is the inside of the place." He unrolled another sheet of drawings and as she studied the tentative plans she realised that this venture was something into which he had put a lot of time and effort. For himself, of course, she reminded herself. Suddenly she had a crazy impulse to touch the thick dark head as he bent over the designs. Jerking herself back to sanity, she tried to concentrate on what he was saying.

"Each unit to have separate kitchen, bedroom, bathroom, lounge ... We can decide on colour schemes later. Okay with you?"

She nodded.

"And this is how I see the restaurant. Separate from the main building, but you reach it by a covered thatched walkway amongst the trees. The thatched roofing is for when it rains –"

"Rain – here? I can't imagine it!" She was thinking how attractive he was at the moment, intent on his project, so that she could gaze at him to her heart's content. At that moment he glanced upwards and she wrenched her thoughts aside.

"Does it rain? Ever heard of a tropical downpour, Robyn? You'll be surprised one of these days!"

She laughed and attempted to concentrate on the detailed sketch.

"It'll be open, bamboo pillars with climbing plants, looking out over the lagoon. I picture it with native-style decor – coconut matting on the floor, walls hung with tapa-cloth, lights shining through big conch shells –"

"And Bula –"

"You don't think I'd forget him!"

They laughed together and he rolled up the stiff papers. "I'll get on to all this right away. You'll be lucky being in one of the bures, with all the hammering and tearing down that's going to go on around here next week, but the sooner it's started the better."

"Yes, of course." He would of course be in a hurry to get his money back from the venture. You couldn't blame him for that.

"Now it's your turn," he smiled, and twisted a rubber band around the roll of papers. "You were going to show me the mural for the restaurant?"

"I'll go and get it."

The long picture was awkward to carry, but she brought it to the verandah. David came to meet her at the foot of the steps and held it up at arm's length while he studied the canvas. "You've got it, Robyn!" Enthusiasm tinged his tone. "That translucent under-water colour that isn't like anything else on earth! And this stylised form of coral and sea-plants and tortoise is just what I had in mind – only I never thought I'd be lucky enough to find anyone who could carry it out! Are you working on anything at the moment?"

Once again his genuine interest in her work served to put other matters from her mind. She said eagerly, "I've got an idea for the painting of a child, a native child. Selani, that's my nice Fijian maid, says her family live in the nearest village. She tells me I can take a walk over there any time and have a model all ready-made. It seems her married sister lives in the village with her husband and their two small boys." Without realising the implications of what she was saying, she ran on, "I'm thinking of going over there this afternoon."

"Good! I'll take you."

"You don't need to. I mean ... I can easily find the way by myself ..." At the teasing glimmer in his eyes her voice faltered into silence. Well, it wasn't her fault that he insisted on coming with her, she told herself defensively. She'd tried to dissuade him so Johnny needn't think – Oh dear, why was she worrying about Johnny's opinion? He wasn't even here. It didn't matter to him what she did. Only somehow it did matter – a lot. It was dreadful to feel torn in two directions. She knew she shouldn't go with David Kinnear, or at least if she did go, she shouldn't feel so wildly happy about the idea.

They lunched with Eve Daley, and to Robyn's dismay the

81

older woman had to let out the fact that Johnny had been absent from the Islander for almost two weeks. Not that David made any comment, but she knew he wouldn't let her off that lightly. He didn't. For as they took a path winding amongst the palms he turned towards her, asking without preamble, "Why didn't you tell me that your brother had taken off? That he hasn't been around since I was last here?"

She stole a glance, but it told her nothing. "I didn't think," she said lamely, "that you'd be interested."

"*Interested!*" He meant because of the debt, of course.

"Leaving you alone here to cope with everything, including the coral boat. So it wasn't because of the art work that you've been out so much in the boat lately. You took it out because your brother wasn't here to do the job."

"I enjoyed it," she protested swiftly. "Honestly, it's something I've always wanted to do, learn to handle a motor boat. It was fun!" She added a trifle belatedly, "Besides, I wanted to get all the views of the coral I could, for future pictures."

"What's he doing with himself anyway?" She might have known she couldn't fool him one little bit. He wasn't the type of man from whom one could hide things, unfortunately. Such a lazy voice, yet he never missed a thing. Still she struggled determinedly on.

"He'll be away working, trying to help you by getting some cash in hand –"

"Did he tell you that?"

"No, but I just . . . know."

He eyed her consideringly. "You're a nice kid, Robyn, but trying to protect your brother only makes you a lot more vulnerable. He's old enough to look after himself, wouldn't you say?"

She pretended not to understand. "Oh yes, yes! That's why he's away, probably somewhere at sea. Working . . . doing his best," she added wildly.

All at once he appeared to have lost interest in the subject of Johnny. "Ever seen a breadfruit tree? There's one right over your head."

82

She had been too involved in her own affairs to notice that they had entered a dusty pathway curving between high spreading trees. The green branches met overhead. "Or tapioca?"

"Never!"

"You've seen nothing yet! Look over there! What does that look like to you?"

She followed his glance towards the indentation by the side of the path where grass grew over a cluster of great flat stones. "Just a pit of some sort —"

"It's one that's been used by the firewalkers at some time or other, by the look of it. They come from their own island of Beqa. Ever heard of them, Rob?"

She nodded, only too happy to forget personal problems. "Johnny told me about them . . . but I still can't believe anyone could walk bare-footed on white-hot stones and not feel a thing —"

"It's true! Just one of those mystical affairs the scientists can't find any explanation for." They strolled on along a road cut through the jungle rising on either side. As they went on, David, carrying her sketching materials, pointed out to her the various trees with their tropical fruits, the metal bands high on the coconut trees that had been put there to combat the rats. Somehow Robyn thought she had never known a two-mile walk pass so effortlessly and enjoyably.

At last they emerged from the filtered light of the jungle in sight of the coast. The tide had receded, leaving an expanse of flat silver sea and gleaming sand. They rounded a point and quite suddenly they came in sight of a grassy clearing with its clusters of native bures. Fijian men were busy stripping the fibre from coconut palms and putting up foundations for new huts. Not far from a large thatched hut, women were seated on the grass weaving mats from pandanus leaves. Beside them were piled shell ornaments, woven mats, necklaces of beads and dried nuts. The smiling dark-eyed women did not press the sale of their handiwork, but as Robyn paused to admire the local jewellery David said to her, "Which one would you like?"

She chose a long necklace made of tiny shells in shades of browns and amber. "And just for good measure –" he selected a starfish pin cut from shimmering mother-of-pearl and handed it to her. While he paid for the purchases she slipped over her head the bead necklace that blended so well with the natural linen of the short shift she was wearing.

"Selani said her sister lives in a hut right at the end of the village," she told David as they strolled over the short grass in the direction of a line of thatched bures.

It was dark inside the hut and for a moment Robyn had difficulty in focusing her gaze. Then, moving over the mat on the earthen floor, she caught sight of a smiling big-framed Fijian woman and two small, wide-eyed boys. An open fire glowed at one end of the hut and nearby were cooking pots, a scoured and spotless frying pan.

The children ran at once to their mother, burying their faces in her voluminous long cotton skirt, and miraculously David produced from a shirt pocket a small bag of sweets.

"Hello, little one!" Bending down to the child, Robyn cradled the dark-eyed toddler in her arms. Lustrous eyes gazed back at her and the small boy gave her a shy smile. Looking up at that moment, Robyn surprised an unexpected expression of tenderness – there was no mistaking it – in David's eyes, and suddenly self-conscious she put the child down and rose to her feet.

She turned to the big Fijian woman. "You wouldn't mind if I made a picture of your little boys? Just a quick one. They're such lovely children."

"Not mind, but keeping them both still," she burst into a fit of giggles that reminded Robyn of Selani. Then, scooping up both children, she seated herself and settled the boys on her capacious lap.

Robyn took up her sketch-pad. "It's just an impression really," she murmured to David as he stood watching her flying pencil. "I can fill in the details later." Soon on the blank paper faces began to emerge. The sweet-faced young Fijian mother; two small brown native boys, wide-eyed with wonder and mercifully too spellbound by the novelty of what was happening to attempt to scamper away.

She had almost completed the swift outlines when a tall good-looking young Fijian man appeared in the opening. Soon he was chatting with the others, explaining to the strangers something of native customs and the way of life in his own village.

"What is the big hut used for?" Robyn enquired, putting away her sketch-pad. "The one all by itself in the village? Does anyone live there?"

"That's the meeting house," the Fijian man informed her. "Once every month we have a meeting there. Everyone from the village comes. We talk, fix up any troubles –"

"Don't tell me," Robyn teased, "that you have problems here in this island paradise?"

"Not many. Just sometimes the boys of the tribe, they think they grown-up, can do as they like. They want to leave the tribal grounds and go to live in the town. Some of them give cheek, but that soon settled –"

Robyn smiled towards David. "They've managed to solve the generation gap problem!" Turning to the Fijian man, she asked, "How on earth do you do it?"

"No problem. Chief of the tribe, he gets out the big stick. He wallop boy good. After that, no more trouble!"

Robyn laughed, "I can imagine!"

Presently, after promising Selani's sister that she would return in a week or two with a sketch of the children, Robyn preceded David through the opening of the thatched hut.

Outside the sky was a moist inky blue and a sudden gust of wind sent a coconut tumbling from a nearby palm. They had gone only a short distance when lightning zig-zagged around them. Almost immediately rain pelted down on their faces. The sea was dark green scattered with a myriad dancing drops and the path streamed with water. "Come on, run for it!" Plucking an umbrella-like pandanus leaf from a nearby bush, David held it over Robyn's head as they hurried

85

towards the nearest hut. His arm was still around her as laughing and breathless, they fell in at the opening and stood peering around the empty dwelling. A fire still glowed in the grate on the floor, so evidently the owners weren't far distant.

Robyn drew herself free, but she was still very much aware of his nearness. "How long ... will it last ... the rain, do you think?"

He brushed the drops of moisture from her hair. The look in his eyes as they rested on her said quite plainly: Quite a while, I hope. Aloud he murmured reassuringly, "Not long. These tropical downpours soon rain themselves out. Why, Robyn? Don't you like being here?"

"It's awfully hot," she said breathlessly, "what with the fire ... and everything."

"Why don't you come right out with it," for a moment the lazy tones deceived her, "admit you don't like being shut up with the enemy?"

"But you're not ... my enemy." Her voice was very low.

"Good! That's a start anyway. I told you it was start-again time! Robyn –" The intensity of his gaze ... magnetism ... electricity ... drew her towards him and once again she felt his mouth on hers. This time his kiss wasn't gentle, only ... deeply satisfying, wildly exciting.

At last she came back to the present. "David –"

"That's better," his voice was tender. "I've wanted –" He stopped short as a fuzzy dark head appeared in the opening and a small Fijian boy peered towards them. "There's a man looking for you. Here he comes now, in the car."

"Thanks, son." They moved towards the opening, but the child had already sped away in the direction of a nearby hut.

Robyn took a deep breath. "It's Johnny! He's come looking for me!"

"What of it? Relax, honey, he's not going to worry me any."

"I know, but –"

A car door slammed outside and the next minute Johnny entered the hut. Robyn glanced up to meet his brooding gaze.

86

Angrily he dashed the raindrops from his face and she realised that her apprehensions were well justified. He looked furious, his grey eyes stormy, his mouth tightly set.

"Hello." Her smile wavered, but she kept it plastered to her features. "Were you looking for me?"

"I was," he said sulkily, ignoring the other man. "Eve told me you'd gone over to Selani's sister's place to sketch the kids. We thought you'd be drenched. If I'd known you weren't alone, I wouldn't have bothered."

"If *I'd* known you were coming back today, I wouldn't have come here at all." She hated herself for the conciliatory note in her voice.

"Well, you'd better jump into the car now," he said ungraciously. "Coming, Kinnear?"

"No, thanks. The rain's almost over and I could do with a stroll."

"Suit yourself. Coming, Rob?"

She hesitated, said tentatively to David, "You don't — mind?"

His grin was as lazy as ever. "Why should I? After bending over the old drawing boards a lot of the time a good tramp is just what I like — Oh, Johnny, you'll find the plans for the alterations on a desk in my room. Run your eye over them when you get back, will you? I'd like to have your say-so before I give the builders the green light to go ahead."

The young face hardened. "Do as you please. It's over to you now."

"Okay, then," David said in his pleasant *unshakeable* tone. "So long as you're around when the place is fixed up into working order and you're back in business. I'll get the workmen started next week. After that a month should do it. Just wanted to make sure you approved —"

"Why ask me? Go right ahead! So far as I'm concerned I don't care what you do, so long as you restrict your activities to the house!" His significant glance swept to Robyn and she felt hot with embarrassment.

How could Johnny behave like this, even though he had

87

some provocation, goodness knows! For a man of his independent nature, it must be galling to be forced to account to someone else for your movements in your own home. Only Johnny wasn't behaving as though the old Islander were his home – her swift thoughts chased one another through her mind. He acted as though the guesthouse was the last place he wanted to be in, especially if the architect were to be there as well!

Sick with humiliation, she didn't glance towards David but made her way out into the teeming rain. She splashed through a puddle and seated herself in the car beside Johnny. They shot forward in a shower of spray, past the small pond with its pink and white waterlilies floating on the surface, that was rapidly filling. But she was aware only of Johnny's thunderous face. She wanted to ask him where he had been lately and why he hadn't contracted her, but something in his set look deterred her. A few short weeks ago she wouldn't have hesitated, yet now ... Surely she wasn't afraid of Johnny, her brother, even in his dark moods.

"I thought you had more sense," he burst out, "traipsing all over the place with *him*!"

"It was only a walk," she pointed out mildly.

"I wouldn't trust Kinnear anywhere!"

"Anyway," she asked, "where were you all week? I was worried about you at first, until Eve told me you often took off for days at a time without letting anyone know."

It was the wrong thing to say, she realised almost at once. He flung her a scowling glance. "Now *you're* trying to tie me down – Sorry, Sis," the endearing lopsided smile lightened the young face, "you'll have to get used to my wandering ways. I never thought you'd take it to heart ... I would have sent you a message, but I was away on a cruise boat and we didn't touch any port for a week." Somehow she felt it was a lie, but it wasn't worth arguing about.

As suddenly as it had come, the brief tropical storm was over. Birds began singing on bedraggled branches and over the mountains the sky was a drenched blue. The humid atmosphere had lightened and palms and jungle growth glittered with raindrops. Now David would be able to make his way back to the guest house.

Aloud she said, "You were pretty awful to David just now."

"I can be a lot worse than that, as he'll soon find out if I have to put up with much more of his interference. Not that it's likely. After today I won't be around much at the Islander."

With a sinking heart she glanced towards his stormy face. "You mean —"

"It all depends how things turn out. I'll tell you one thing, though, Rob. When I do come back here, it will be on my own terms, not *his*!"

"I don't know what you mean." Suddenly her feelings got the better of her. "Don't you care about all the money we owe —"

He threw her a wry sideways glance. "You'd be surprised, Sis. Actually at the moment it's about the only thing in the world I do care about! You'll just have to take my word for it, believe me, when I say I'll settle the score with Kinnear, right to the last cent, but it's got to be *in my own way!*"

"But you won't tell me how —"

"You'll know before very long, one way or the other."

"I wish you wouldn't be so mysterious. What can I tell Pam? She's rung up twice while you've been away, once on long-distance from Australia, wanting to know when you'd be back."

His face hardened. "So what? Just tell her that I don't know. It all depends on what I'm doing and where I happen to be."

They had reached the grounds of the guesthouse and he pulled up with a jerk at the foot of the steps. As she got out of the car he revved the engine. "'Bye!" A defiant wave of his hand and the small old car was speeding down the driveway.

As she watched the vehicle vanish around a bend screened by thickly-growing banana palms, Robyn was conscious of mixed feelings. She was struck by a niggling feeling of disloyalty. Going over to the enemy camp — was that the way it would look to Johnny? Was it because he had come across her and David together today that her brother wasn't staying on at the Islander? All the same, he needn't have behaved quite so unpleasantly towards David. I'll see him and apologise for what Johnny said today, she promised herself. The minute David gets back to the house I'll find him and tell him that Johnny didn't mean what he said. It's just his way.

She had showered and changed into dry shirt and shorts and was moving out to the verandah to wait for him when David came striding along the passage. "Oh, Robyn, I was just coming to look for you —" Who would dream from his cheerful, offhanded manner that such a short time ago he and she — She brought up her random thoughts with a jerk.

"I'm off now," he was saying. "Be back some time when things start moving down here."

"David —" She took a step towards him, then hesitated.

"What is it?"

"Just —" At that moment a group of fishermen pushed past them in the narrow corridor. There was no opportunity for private conversation, no chance to say "I'm sorry". She turned away. "It doesn't matter."

"Tell me when I come back. 'Bye." He was gone, taking the steps two at a time, swinging around on the grass below to send her a friendly wave, just as though she hadn't allowed her brother to be so insulting to him. Was it for her sake that David put up with such a lot from Johnny? She couldn't think of another reason, yet she couldn't really accept that one! The turning car blurred out of focus as the foolish tears misted her eyes. How could a kiss make all that difference, leave her with this aching sense of regret? If Johnny hadn't come seeking her, if she hadn't agreed to return with him in his car, would David be leaving here so soon, so *uncaringly*? Suddenly the time when the builders would move in to begin renovations on the motel seemed an awfully long period ahead!

CHAPTER V

THE days slipped by and there was no further word from Johnny. In view of the bitter resentment her brother had displayed towards David at their last meeting, Robyn wasn't really surprised. She could only hope that once the place was remodelled and again in full working order, Johnny would think better of David; change his attitude of high-handed defiance.

"Don't worry about your brother being away so much of the time," Eve Daley told her cheerfully, "it happens all the time." But Robyn couldn't help the small niggle of anxiety. On the shabby desk in the dining room two letters addressed to Johnny and bearing an Australian postmark awaited him.

"Those will be from Pam," Mrs. Daley said. "It's too bad, those two being parted like this, and all over some stupid misunderstanding, I'll be bound. Pam's crazy about him and I was sure that Johnny felt the same way about her. He's a fool if he lets her go, a nice girl like that, and I told him so too! Pam isn't the type of girl to go on trying to patch things up for ever!"

Robyn knew a moment's pity for the other girl, trying so desperately to put a lost love out of mind, then weakening and writing a letter to Johnny. Receiving no reply, she had written a second time, hoping ... Probably by now she despaired of ever receiving an answer.

"They say in Suva," the older woman murmured, "that Johnny and Noeline are always together these days. I never thought she would take him back, not after what happened. I simply can't understand it."

"Maybe she still cares for him." Robyn could imagine what had happened. A proud wealthy girl in love with a man who possessed little beyond a decrepit old guesthouse on the Coral Coast. A man who had the effrontery to cancel extensive wedding plans at the last moment. Johnny had told her that he would manage his problems *his own way*. Surely he wouldn't, he couldn't – Feckless and over-optimistic he might be, but to marry a girl he cared little about merely to settle a debt, relieve his intolerable position of being forced into subservience towards a stranger, a man he hated ... Oh no, Johnny wouldn't do that! Even his stubborn pride couldn't lead him to go to those lengths.

Aloud she said, "He's lucky to have two girls so crazy about him."

"Especially," the older woman's significant glance rested on Robyn's thoughtful face, "when *they* both know his failings!"

Oh dear, Robyn thought exasperatedly, she's just like David. She believes too that I'm mistaken about Johnny, but they'll both see how wrong they are. Just give him a little time and he'll prove to them that I'm right.

Meanwhile the time passed in a succession of sun-drenched days. Robyn explored the reef at low tide, collecting shells along the shoreline, lazed and swam in the turquoise waters of the lagoon. Between times she worked on her portrait of the small native boy she had seen in the village or experimented with stylized forms of palm trees and the local outrigger canoes with their matting sails.

"You're getting to be a real islander," Eve Daley told her, her glance resting on Robyn's smoothly-tanned skin, the long fair hair now gilded with a patina of lighter gold.

"Think so?" Robyn laughed. "Then how about letting me help more around the place? Couldn't I do the accounts for you?"

"No need," the capable older woman assured her. "Wait until David gets the alterations done, then there'll be more than enough for both of us to do. Right now you're helping out wonderfully with the coral viewing."

"I suppose." Daily trips out to the reef had now become part of a new way of life. She was accustomed to the controls, the short run out to the waves foaming over the reef.

Whether clear in the sunlight or shadowed by shifting cloud, the ever-changing world of tiny jewelled fish and vibrant coral never failed to fill her with wonder. Somehow too, taking the boat out with tourists gave her a satisfying feeling of working, of doing something towards easing the financial burden that had come to loom so large in her life.

"Who knows," Eve told her, "if you keep on like this you might end up by turning the coral boat into a famous tourist excursion, like the *Olooloo* cruise."

"What's that?"

"It's just about the most popular sea excursion in Suva. A cruiser takes tourists out to the reef. Then skin divers bring up the sea creatures from the deep. A pretty girl in a bikini sits on the deck and explains all about the live coral and fish that the divers pass up to her from the water. The boat makes a short stop at the Tradewinds Hotel, it's built right on the water, then the girl sings and plays her guitar on the way back to the wharves in Suva."

Robyn thought, I could do that, all except the guitar-and-singing bit. Her mind leaped ahead. Later on when the Islander was updated and better known, why not exchange the old *Katrina* for a cruiser? She could serve coffee and refreshments on board, take out a large number of tourists at a time. Finding divers would be easy in a place where the natives were at home in the water. Aloud she said, "I'd like to make that trip. Does the *Olooloo* go every day?"

Mrs. Daley nodded. "Every afternoon from the seafront at Suva. Why don't you go tomorrow? You'd enjoy it. Get a taxi here back afterwards, or if you like you could put up at my place in Suva for the night. There's a crowd of students living there, but they would make you very welcome. I go along whenever I get a chance."

Once again Robyn was struck by the fact that her brother's frequent absences from the guesthouse must throw an extra burden on the older woman's capable shoulders. When could she ever leave the Islander for a night? The thought prompted her to say, "You haven't been away much lately, not at all since I've been here."

The cheerful face remained untroubled. "And that's not long, if you count up, but there's nothing to stop you having a day off."

But there was. She didn't want to be away from the house should David arrive. Somebody had to be around when he returned here with the builders. And if Johnny hadn't returned ... Unconsciously she sighed, telling herself that it was useless basing her movements on David. Already he occupied far too important a place in her thoughts ... and dreams. "I'll go tomorrow, after I've made the coral trip, and if the architect does come, well, I'll be back that night, or early the next day."

The Indian driver guided his taxi carefully around the hairpin bends of the rough metal road as he followed the Queens Road cutting between dense jungle-clad hills. At length when Robyn had decided there couldn't surely be any further curves on the route they swept along a straight stretch and came in sight of a wide blue harbour ringed with mountains. On the hills above the sea, white-painted houses gleamed amidst surrounding trees and bush. Soon they were moving towards the busy seaport with its profusion of yachts and catamarans, cruisers and overseas cargo boats. Accompanied by a constant tooting of the horn, the driver negotiated a bend, skilfully avoiding oncoming cars and trucks, swept into the main traffic, to draw up in the main street of Suva, the most colourful and cosmopolitan city of the South Pacific.

She paid the driver, then stood looking around her. Taxis were pulling in all along the seafront and the *Olooloo* rocked gently at her berth amongst the cluster of yachts and pleasure craft on the sheltered water. Reflecting that she had half an hour to spare before the departure of the tourist excursion, Robyn strolled along the wide main street shaded by an avenue of towering banyan trees. She paused to glance in at the windows of a modern store where a variety of high fashion imported clothing was attractively displayed. Nearby was a

Chinese café, then a cluster of small bazaar-like stores with their exotic world of duty-free goods at low prices. There were cameras, jewellery, masks, perfume and yards of beautiful silk sarees and material, all printed in tropical designs in the alive-o colours of the South Pacific. A glance up a narrow byway showed her dingy dark shops where Indian tailors were busily treading sewing machines and craftsmen were weaving mats. It was all colourful and different. If only it wasn't also steamingly, humidly HOT! She pushed the hair back from her damp forehead and crossing the main street made her way towards the markets.

The strong smell of market produce, seafoods and fresh fish met her as she entered the dim interior with its long stalls and narrow crowded passageways. The air was filled with the chatter of Indian and Chinese merchants and huge coconut baskets were piled high with yams, taro, sea-snails and crabs. Native children extended great wedges of glistening watermelon to thirsty shoppers and Fijians stood behind towering displays of fresh bananas and pineapples.

Making her way through the jostling crowd of mixed races moving along the narrow space between benches piled high with produce and woven baskets, she paused at a native stall to purchase a pair of woven scuffs with their gay crimson pom-poms.

"Robyn!" A sense of excitement shot along her nerves. Only one man she knew possessed that particular lazy timbre in his deep tones. Only one man could flutter her pulses with just one word! She swung around to face David, his smile as heart-warming as ever, just as though it were the most natural thing in the world that they two should run into each other in the native markets. Pushing through the throng, he reached her side and all at once the babel of voices, the crowded long stalls weren't noisy and odoriferous and bewildering any more but exotic and colourful, a day touched with magic. It's seeing someone you know when you're in a strange city, she rationalized to herself in an effort to explain away the sudden wild excitement that was flooding her senses.

"Come on," he took the scuffs from her and stuffed them in the pocket of his tan cotton shorts. "Let me get you something. A souvenir? Everyone buys souvenirs at the market." Taking her arm, he piloted her through the milling throng. "Pearls? Beads? No? A bunch of bananas, then, just off the tree. Dried fish? Taro?"

She laughed up into his face. "Definitely not taro –"

"Have you ever tried it?"

"No, but –"

"How can you tell, then? That's the trouble with you, Robyn, you lack the spirit of adventure! How about these?" He guided her towards a great mound of ripe pineapples, golden, luscious and mouth-watering in the overpowering heat. "Only a few cents! A bargain if ever I saw one! You will?"

"Mmm, I'm so thirsty!"

"You'll get it in a minute, when we're on the way out. I'm not carrying that monstrous fruit in my pocket, even for you, Rob. Wait, I've got it! A basket! How about that?" He indicated a nearby stall with its assortment of cane merchandise. "Made on the premises, only the best pandanus leaf used, latest style –"

"Look, who's doing the selling around here?"

"All right then, you choose one!" She strolled along the bench. "Can I have this one, David?" The feather-light basket wasn't a large one but definitely attractive with its decoration of pink and white and brown shells.

When he had paid the smiling Fijian stall owner, they strolled on, listening to the mixture of foreign voices, intrigued by the colourful scene around them.

"Now this you could do with –" He paused at a small stall with its assortment of woven sun-hats.

"How about yourself?" Robyn laughed back.

"Why not?" Taking a wide woven sombrero from a big Fijian woman, he placed it at a rakish angle over his tanned face. "Like it?"

Smilingly, head on one side, she studied him. "Uh-huh,

there's a gorgeous shell ornament on one side."

"You're hedging. Let's see how it would look on you!" Very gently he slipped the sunglasses from her eyes and placed the hat over her bright hair.

She laughed, looking up at him.

"Keep it, Rob, it's just the thing for the *Olooloo* cruise —"

She stopped laughing and stared at him, lips parted in surprise. "Now just how did you guess that I was —" But he was paying the plump Fijian woman standing on the opposite side of the stall.

Admit it, she told herself. It's just wonderful to be going on the excursion with David! Awful how she kept forgetting that she shouldn't like him so much, feel so happy whenever she found herself in his company. But it was merely an outing, nothing of any importance, so why not make the most of the hot, sunshiny day?

"Let's get out of this mob," he was saying. A hand placed on her smooth tanned arm and he was guiding her through the throng of Indians, Fijians, and overseas tourists. Out in the open again they strolled along the seafront where Indian taxi-drivers were pulling up at the wharves and tourists were gathering near the various excursion vessels.

Although the glass-bottomed cruiser was rocking gently on sun-dappled water, the gangplank was not yet up. They dropped down on the wharf steps in the sunshine and David, taking a knife from his pocket, sliced the fresh pineapple, cutting away the prickly skin. The cool fruit with its sweet tangy flavour was thirst-quenching and delicious. Afterwards they joined the group of tourists who were moving over the gangplank to the cruiser with its gay blue pennant, *Olooloo*, fluttering at the masthead.

"What does the name mean?" Robyn asked as they strolled along the deck.

"Can't you guess? Say it slowly. *O ... loo ... loo ...* the sound of doves." The soft haunting music of native guitars followed them as they moved along the deck beneath a canvas awning.

With relief she realised that he hadn't asked the question she dreaded. "Is Johnny back at the house yet?" Perhaps he had given up asking.

A smiling Jijian crew welcomed them aboard and soon they were moving over the rippling blue sea. Presently the engines were cut and they drifted over the coral reef that made the water here free from sharks. They watched from the deck as youthful Fijian skin-divers dropped over the side, surfacing to bring with them from the deep, clusters of coral. A pretty native girl in a coral-pink bikini arranged the treasure from the sea on a small platform, then held up for observation a tropical jewelled fish before placing it in a small tank of sea-water with other tiny fish. Heads craned eagerly forward and Robyn slipped from her shoulder the leather case holding her Instamatic. In the crowd pressing around her on all sides she found it impossible to view the exhibit the native girl was holding up until all at once David cleared a space for her and propelled her gently forward.

His tone was perfectly normal, so why was she so over-whelmingly aware of his nearness? How could you focus your gaze on a rubbery starfish when all you could think of was David's arm around you, his breath on your face? Blindly she clicked the shutter, then realised that he had no intention of releasing her until she had taken further shots. How could he guess the way in which he was affecting her? In quick succession she snapped a striped yellow-and-black butterfly fish, a coral-encrusted wine bottle and a puffer fish, an incredible sea creature with the strange ability to blow itself up when danger threatened until it resembled a baby's pink head.

"Did you ever –" Swinging around to David, she found she couldn't quite meet that bright gaze.

At length the skin-divers climbed aboard the cruiser, the attractive native girl threw fish and coral back into the deep and the throng of onlookers dispersed over the decks. The next moment engines throbbed into life and the cruiser was moving across the harbour in the direction of the Tradewinds Hotel, where the sea lapped against the dining room. A few steps over the floating jetty, then they were entering the Quarterdeck Restaurant with its wide balcony looking out over the sun-flecked water. Alongside, famous ocean-going yachts were tied up at the Anchorage Bar and a fleet of small craft moored nearby waited to take visitors by water-taxi to Suva.

David chose a nearby table and ordered drinks. They came served by a Fijian girl with a hibiscus in her hair and a wide and friendly smile. The drinks were cool and frosted with a lilac orchid clinging to the side of each tall glass. Robyn sipped idly, her gaze moving over the scattered atolls of the harbour, then back towards the luxury craft moored so close. "Dreamy island setting. You know, there must be some famous international yachts tied up here. Just look at that super one —" Her voice trailed away as a group appeared on deck, amongst them Johnny and a slight, sandy-haired young woman. A few moments later the two were strolling over the jetty towards them. Robyn, taking in the immaculate outfit of white slacks and nautical blue and white striped sweater, mused that for all the expensive garments and exquisite grooming, the other girl presented a painfully nondescript appearance.

Johnny appeared as surprised as herself at the unexpected encounter. For a few seconds he seemed at a loss for words, then the old rakish grin crossed his bronzed features. "Rob! What on earth are you doing here? No, don't tell me, let me guess! You're on the *Olooloo* cruise, I bet! This is Noeline . . . my sister Robyn . . . David Kinnear."

Coolly assessing greenish eyes, cold as river pebbles, met Robyn's smiling greeting. Somehow she had pictured the girl who Johnny had once cared for enough to want to marry as someone poised and attractive or, at the very least, pretty. What special quality could have drawn Johnny to this plain, sandy-haired girl with the discontented, pettish twist to her thin lips? Only . . . money? The thought came unbidden and she thrust it aside.

Johnny was talking excitedly, almost as though he were trying to avoid an awkward pause or a question.

"Care to join us?" David asked in his affable tones.

"Sorry," Johnny answered quickly, "but we're due to sail in half an hour and time's running out."

"Pity," David observed easily, "I've got the plans all drawn up for the Islander alterations. They're just waiting for your okay before I get the builders on the job and we're away!"

In a moment Johnny's face had changed, all the light-hearted laughter wiped away. "Another time –"

"But, Johnny –" Noeline laid a thin, freckled hand on his arm.

"It doesn't matter," he told her. "It's nothing of any importance." Swinging around to David, he said in tense, angry voice, "Like I told you before, do as you like! You will anyway, so why keep on about it?"

"You're the owner, mate."

"I'm not the only one! Seeing you two are so friendly," there was an ugly twist to Johnny's lips, "why don't you get Robyn on the job instead?"

"I'll do that," David said quietly.

With no alteration in his even tone he had succeeded in putting Johnny firmly in his place, Robyn reflected, and his place at the moment was very definitely that of an ill-tempered, vindictive small boy. How could he be so insufferable?

"Go right ahead!" Robyn noticed the high flush on his cheekbones, "and good luck! Come on, Noeline, time to go!"

Sick with humiliation, Robyn watched the other two as they threaded their way through the small tables. "He looked as if he'd a bit too much to drink," she offered lamely, "and besides, it must have made him furious seeing me ... with you. I mean, he'd never believe that we ran across each other by accident."

"Do *you* believe it, Robyn?"

At last she was forced to meet his smiling gaze. "I never dreamed –"

"I have, often! That's why when I got through to the

Islander this morning and Mrs. Daley told me where you were heading for in Suva –"

"I might have known!" But the next moment other thoughts crowded in, the anxious mortifying recollection of Johnny's behaviour that drove everything else from mind. "Now he'll think – he'll think –"

"What does it matter what he thinks?" David laid a firm brown hand over her fingers. He added with his unshakeable good humour, "Too bad if he takes off. I'll have to make do with you instead for giving me a go-ahead with the plans. Not that I mind, you understand?"

But she was too humiliated by Johnny's behaviour to listen to what he was saying. Thoughtfully she stirred the long cool drink with a sugar-cane swizzlestick. She said uncertainly, "He could be working on that yacht. You know? One of the crew?" Her tone gained confidence. "He often goes away like that, signs on a boat for a trip around the islands."

His voice was very gentle. "Haven't you noticed the name, Rob?"

She followed his gaze to the luxuriously appointed white yacht riding at anchor so close beside them. How could she have failed to see the black letters of *Noeline*?

"Oh!" There wasn't much else she could say. After a moment she murmured, "Wasn't that the girl who Johnny was going to marry, only he changed his mind right at the last moment before the wedding?"

"So they tell me. I wasn't here at the time. I shouldn't imagine a girl would forgive that sort of treatment, but apparently they're the best of friends now. Would *you* overlook a thing like that? Take him back, just as though nothing had happened?"

"Perhaps," Robyn said very low, "nothing else would matter, if I cared enough."

He grinned his easy grin. "Could be it's love – or revenge."

"Revenge?" She was startled out of her thoughts. "What do you mean?"

"Nothing. Forget it. Just a crazy idea that ran through my

101

head. I'm probably way off the beam. Anyway, what does it matter? Forget about Johnny, shall we? He's not really all that important in our scheme of things."

"Oh, but he is!"

"Think so?" His gaze was all at once tender. It said quite plainly that where her brother was concerned, she was very young and stupid ... and vulnerable.

Soon it was time to reboard the excursion boat, but for Robyn a little of the magic of the day had slipped away. She kept remembering Johnny, and wondering. Watching the water rippling around them, she reflected that Johnny hadn't confided to Noeline the true position in regard to his financial losses. To the other girl he was a young man who owned a more or less prosperous guesthouse. Something else concerning the other two worried her, and at last she pinpointed it. Something was missing in their relationship, she sensed it. There was no real feeling between them ... she knew she wasn't mistaken ... so why ... Of course there was no accounting for love, but she had an inner conviction that love didn't enter into their relationship. Convenience perhaps, advantages on Johnny's side financially. What was it that David had suggested? Revenge, but that was absurd. One thing, she had no need any more to make excuses for her brother's absence from the guesthouse. It was all too clear to David that Johnny preferred enjoying himself in the company of people to whom money was no problem, rather than pulling his weight to retrieve the position in his own property. To ease her conscience, she said suddenly to David, leaning on the rail at her side, "Maybe I will look over those plans. I mean, if Johnny isn't around to okay them —"

"And mightn't be for quite a while."

"I didn't say that —"

"I did, but never mind," for her face had fallen despairingly, "you'll do, Robyn. After all, you're the other half of the partnership."

Her heart gave a sudden lurch, then she realised that of course he wasn't referring to himself but to Johnny.

"We can take a run over them when we get back," he was saying.

As the cruiser moved towards Suva harbour Robyn eyed the attractive native girl who had explained and exhibited the findings of the divers out at the reef. Now it appeared that her duties were over, for she was perched on the deck rail, her brown fingers plucking the strings of her guitar while her strong sweet voice rose in a foot-tapping rhythm that was joined by the passengers.

David had left his car parked on the wharves and soon they were driving through the wide, colourful streets. They dined in a small Chinese café and when they emerged into the street the heat met them. Guiding the car out of the city, David took a steep hill overlooking the harbour where old homes and new apartment blocks were screened amongst the tropical greenery of trees and bushes.

Outside a high block of modern units he braked to a stop and soon they were climbing a flight of stairs. He turned the key in a lock and they were in a spacious lounge room, delightfully cool with air-conditioning after the humidity outside. Softly lighted, the room was furnished in tonings of browns and golds. A man's room, she thought, glancing around her as he went to a desk and picking up a roll of blueprints brought them back to a low table. He indicated a low chair, then held a light to her cigarette. "Now you can get some idea of how the finished place will look." He spread out the detailed drawing. "Here's the pool, bang in front of the entrance. I don't want to do anything to interfere with the natural environment, so we'll have it here. That way we won't have to cut down more than a couple of palms."

Robyn studied the outspread plan, then glanced up in amazement. "But you've made the pool turtle-shaped!"

"Of course. That's what you wanted, wasn't it?"

"Oh yes, but it was only a suggestion."

"A good one! Round the edge of the pool I thought we'd have lots of hibiscus bushes, all in one shade."

"Lemon yellow?"

"Couldn't be better! And over here by the entrance, an open porch shaded by hanging purple orchids. The modern units will be scattered amongst the coconut palms. They'll look like bures, but inside they'll be the last word in comfort and convenience. The old ones can be pulled down, they've had their day. Now over here is where I propose to place the restaurant." He came to stand beside her, bending over her shoulder as he indicated a place on the plan.

"I see." It was very hard to follow his warm tones when his dark head was so close to her own and her foolish heart was thud-thudding so hard she was terrified he would hear it. All she knew was that the proposed project, blending in with natural surroundings, would be probably the most attractively designed building on the Coral Coast ... and that he was much too near her at the moment for her to be able to make any clear judgement. With an effort she dragged her whirling thoughts back to his enthusiastic voice.

"I'm planning the new restaurant as a dine-and-dance place in native decor, with a separate snack bar for odd meals. Staff will be no problem with all the labour that's available here and for the key-line position, I'm counting on a friend of mine to take over as hostess-receptionist. Maria's tied up looking after a chalet-type outfit in Switzerland at the moment, but she's promised to take on the job at the Islander just as soon as we're ready for her. Actually," his voice warmed, "we're in luck to get anyone of Maria's calibre. She's a fluent linguist too, and that counts for a lot in a place like this where a French tourist may be giving a meal order to a Fijian waiter, to be prepared by an Indian chef! If anyone can manage staff problems and keep things on an even footing, she can. You'll like her!"

Already Robyn had a feeling that Maria wouldn't be one of her favourite people, though it was clear that in David's opinion there was no one to equal her. Probably there wasn't — in her own sphere. Did she mean a lot to him in a personal sense as well? His pleasant smiling face as usual gave nothing away, but she had an uneasy presentiment that Maria's arrival wasn't going to make her own invidious position at the Islander any easier.

"Is she . . . pretty?" The words were past her lips before she could stop to think.

His quizzical glance rested on Robyn's downcast face, and she knew he had noted the pink that was flooding her face. "I think so." He stubbed the ash from his cigarette. "Her husband was a particular mate of mine."

She glanced up at him in surprise. "Was?"

"Keith was killed in an accident last year in the Alps. That's why I've been keen to get Maria here to take over. Might get her mind off Keith . . . give her a fresh interest."

Waspishly Robyn found herself hoping that the other girl's interest wasn't centred in David himself. A dark tide of jealousy, sharp and bewildering, attacked her. Absurd to imagine that a man in his early thirties wouldn't have women friends; in all probability a special one he was fond of. He could please himself, couldn't he, in regard to feminine company, and no doubt he did! Maria would be older, sophisticated, someone with whom he would feel at ease. Not a young girl who felt younger still when she was with him, and had no talent for smart conversation or quick repartee with which to counter his teasing remarks.

"What do you think of it all?" His voice jerked her from her unhappy thoughts.

"Fabulous! I've got an idea of my own too to tell you about. That's why I went on the cruise today, to get an idea as to how it's done."

"How do you mean?" He was regarding her with his lazy stare.

"Oh, it's a big idea I've dreamed up." He was listening attentively now, she realised as she ran on. "It's a bit of a long-term plan, but when the place is all done up I thought we could get a much bigger boat than the old *Katrina*, one large enough to take a crowd, about the size of the one we were on today. Then we could take the other hotel tourists as well as our own guests on regular excursions out to the reef. I could act the part like the girl we saw today. I could do everything she did, except the musical part. All I'd need would be a couple of bikinis – and a nice smile! There are lots of natives around who could do the diving for coral. Don't you think it's a good idea, David?"

"No!" She had never seen him so roused. All unwittingly, it had seemed, she had crashed that cool composure. "I wouldn't hear of it."

"*You* wouldn't!"

"That's what I said! Make no mistake about it, Rob, that notion of yours is out – definitely! You can put the idea right out of your head. I wouldn't allow you to do it!"

"But it has nothing to do with you!"

"It has, you know."

"Oh yes ... thanks for reminding me." The dark despairing expression that could come so suddenly darkened her averted face.

"Be sensible, Rob. It wouldn't work."

"Sensible!" All at once she was nettled. Why should she allow herself to be ordered about in this high-handed fashion? "I don't see why not," she persisted stubbornly. "I think it's a real brainwave. Imagine all the dollars it would bring in!"

"It wouldn't, you know. Look at it this way. A cruiser of that type would cost a packet. It would take years to get the cost back in excursion fares. Oh, it's all right in Suva, of course, where they get the tourists from overseas liners, but out at the coast where it's more or less isolated, it would be a different story. Anyway, I wouldn't allow you –"

"*What* did you say?" She stared up at him, eyes bright with defiance.

"You heard, Rob. I wouldn't dream of letting you in for a job like that."

"Other people do it."

"Other people are trained for the work. They know how to handle the situation, any situation –"

"And I suppose," she suggested bitterly, "that I don't?"

"Forget it. If you're thinking along those lines, it's out!"

While she was casting about in her mind for a sufficiently crushing reply, he added carelessly, "Anyway, the position doesn't arise. I've other plans for you, Rob."

"Such as?"

For a moment he was silent, his gaze resting on her flushed face. "I'll let you know . . . later. But for now, if you've made up your mind to be a working woman, what's wrong with taking over the craft shop?"

She stared across at him in amazement. "But I don't know a thing about shop work!"

"You'd learn quickly enough. That artistic ability of yours would be a real asset there. In a couple of months everything will be ready and you can start ordering stock. It's going to work out, Rob, you'll see. We'll make pots of money —"

"For you!"

"And you!" He flicked her nose. "I told you before, you're a funny kid. Don't you want to make a go of things at the Islander?"

She sighed, avoiding his gaze. "In a way."

"Only you'd rather it was Johnny who was doing it?"

His tone was as easy, as friendly as ever, but underneath she was aware of the truth in what he had said. To change the subject she said, "What about the coral boat if I have to take over the shop?"

He shrugged. "Johnny can take over the *Katrina* if he feels like helping out. If he doesn't there are plenty of local native boys who would jump at the chance of making a few dollars." He eyed her downcast face. "You're not mad about the idea, I take it?"

"All right then, I'll do it," she murmured unwillingly. "I haven't much choice in the matter anyway."

"It was your idea to help," he pointed out cheerfully.

"Yes, I know, but . . ." Suddenly it all came to a head. The shock of finding Johnny living in such different circumstances from what he had led her to believe, her shame-making excuses for his behaviour — excuses that she knew hadn't deceived David in the least — and now his ridiculous opposition to the harmless project she had dreamed up. "It's just Johnny," she blurted out in a voice choked with emotion. "You always talk about him in that funny way – Oh, it's not what you say," she was tripping over herself in confusion, "but the way you say it ... as if you didn't trust him to do anything at all!"

"I don't, actually, but don't let it worry you." He spoke in those deceptively easy tones. "I could be all wrong about Brother John. You know something?" He grinned engagingly. "I hope I am."

"But you don't really expect him to pull his weight? You know you don't!"

He put out a hand to touch her, but she jerked herself away. In a low voice she said bitterly, "You haven't really got much faith in either of us, Johnny or me, that's what you really mean, isn't it? It's just a big excuse, not letting me get the new boat and working on it. Just because we got stranded –" She checked herself, realising that "stranded" was an unfortunate way of describing their plight, giving an impression that what had happened had been their own fault instead of a simple accident that no one could foresee. "You really don't think much of either of us, do you?"

He was still smiling, that hateful, unshakeable smile, almost as though her futile efforts to defend the Carlisles amused rather than annoyed him. "You've got it all wrong, little one –"

"And stop treating me like a child!"

"Would you rather I treated you – like this!" She found herself imprisoned in strong arms. Angrily she stared up into his laughing face, then the next moment his kiss sent everything else from mind for the light embrace changed to something roughly tender ... and meaningful ... and heady.

When she could speak, "I guess I asked for that." Her voice was unsteady.

His arms still encircled her waist and he was looking down at her flushed face with an expression she couldn't fathom. Almost ... with tender concern. But when he spoke his voice was low and oddly intent, like that of a man who has himself well in hand. "Come on, child, I'll run you down to a taxi."

It was funny, but she didn't seem to mind him calling her "child" now. Maybe it was because of the way he was looking at her. The outspread plans lay forgotten on the table as they went in silence out of the room and out into the scented darkness of the Pacific night. Robyn said nothing about staying the night at Mrs. Daley's home. In her present turbulent state of mind the thought of a houseful of strangers was unendurable. All she wanted was to get back to the shelter of the Islander, no matter how late when she arrived there.

On the long drive over darkened roads, her thoughts milled endlessly around the man who had just left her. Humiliating enough to be under financial obligations to him. Now she had to admit that he affected her in another, more personal way. Else why was she still burning with anger towards him? Once she had thought that he was someone special, she'd liked him a lot, yet tonight she had been stung into a quarrel that had surprised herself as much as it had him. And it had got her nowhere. For when it came to a matter of arrangements at the remodelled motel, all her arguments and hot anger couldn't alter the fact that he definitely had the say in the running of the place. It was just as Johnny had told her – David was the boss and he meant to assert his authority in no uncertain terms. The dark landscape slid by and all at once she was tired and fed up – and jealous. Now what could have put that idea in her head? How could she be jealous of a woman she had never met, and regarding David, of all men?

But he knows her well and he likes her a lot! You could tell that by his tone of voice when he spoke of her. Obviously he had terrific confidence in her abilities. He would trust Maria to do the right thing for the Islander every time, whereas he regarded *her* efforts to improve the financial position of the guesthouse in a rather different light. Once again he had made her feel useless and where matters of business were concerned, childishly inexperienced.

Why not come right out with it, admit that what was really on her mind was his kiss, his touch, the disturbing nearness that led her to say such silly dumb things when she should be tossing back smart replies! She turned her head towards the outline of dark jungle-clad hills and attempted to dwell on other less personal matters, but it was no use. The smiling face, the warm voice was there in her mind and she could think of nothing but their meeting in Suva and the hours they had spent together.

In the morning when she had slipped into her swim-suit and strolled down the beach, she was surprised to find someone already there. A girl lay motionless, face down on the sands. She looked, Robyn mused, like someone who wanted to be alone with her thoughts – or who was waiting for someone to join her? Something about the figure in the black bikini struck her as familiar. Of course ... Pam. The next moment the other girl jerked to awareness. For a moment an expression of wild hope lighted her dark eyes, then it was gone. "Hi!" Listlessly she lay back on the sand, hands crossed behind her cap of dark hair. "I got in late last night and Eve told me that you'd taken off for Suva. She said you were planning to go on the *Olooloo* cruise. Enjoy it?"

Robyn dropped down at her side. "Oh yes, it was super! And what do you think? David was on the boat too."

Pam raised enquiring dark eyes. "Again?"

"How do you mean?"

"Oh, just that ages ago I happened to run across him in Suva and he told me he was tired of that particular excursion – but of course that was before he met you!"

"Me? He couldn't care less about me. It just ... happened that way."

"Did it?" Pam's derisive smile was disquieting. It raised a question in her mind, but the answer was so incredible it was simply ridiculous.

"Anyway," Robyn went on lightly, "it was fun. The boat called in at Tradewinds and it was heavenly, right on the

110

water's edge. Then we went back to Suva and a native girl sang and played her guitar."

Put into words there was nothing spectacular in the afternoon excursion, at least, not in this part of the world, and certainly not enough to warrant the deep happiness that had coloured the day – until they had quarrelled.

She was unaware of the sudden droop of her lips, the sadness in her transparent face.

"Then you two had an argument?" Pam prompted softly.

Robyn swung around, startled. "How did you know?"

"Just your expression. Don't look like that. You'll make it up again, or he will. It couldn't have been all that important."

"It was – to me. You see," she ran on in a rush of confidence, "I had this fabulous idea of getting a bigger boat, when the place is all modernized, I mean, and I could do just what the native girl does on the *Olooloo* cruise. I know it would be a success."

"But he wouldn't let you?"

"No . . . and the awful part of it is that I can't do a thing about it. Seeing he's in charge of everything now I have to give in whether I want to or not." It was such a relief to speak with someone who was aware of the true position of affairs at the Islander. The injustice of it all swept over her afresh. "It makes me *mad*!"

"Why wouldn't he agree?"

"Oh, I don't know. Some absurd notion he had about it not paying . . . and other things."

"I can make a guess as to what the 'other things' were. And it must have mattered to you quite a bit or you wouldn't be in such a state about it!"

"I'm *not* in a state," Robyn protested hotly. "It's just so unfair!"

Pam gave her sad mocking smile. "Is that what you call it? When is he coming down here again?"

"Don't ask me! When the builders start work here, I suppose. I don't know. And I don't care either!" she said with feeling.

But the other girl wasn't listening. There was an intentness in her glance. "I don't suppose you happened to come across Johnny when you were around the wharves in Suva?"

"I did, actually." Robyn picked up a handful of sand and watched the heavy grains drop through her fingers.

"You don't have to spell it out," Pam said thickly. "I can see from your face that he wasn't alone. It was Noeline, wasn't it? They were off for a cruise with her parents on their palatial yacht?"

Robyn didn't know what to say.

"Oh, I've heard all about it," Pam's voice was unsteady, "but I didn't believe it. You know how it is, you don't believe a thing because you don't want to, yet all the time deep down you know perfectly well that it's true. You keep hoping . . . and hoping . . . thinking that one of these days he'll come back with arms wide open, telling you it was all a mistake and he's loved you all the time – he didn't ask about me?"

Robyn shook her head. "There wasn't time. I only saw him for a minute or so. He – they – were due to sail in half an hour." She was shocked to see the other girl had paled beneath the tan. "I'm sorry, Pam," she murmured awkwardly, "I wish I could do something to help."

Pam tried in vain to steady her trembling lips. "You can't. I've just got to get over him, somehow. It's his being with her that hurts so much. He must have cared for her all along. That's the part I can't take."

"David said it could be revenge?" The words came to her lips unthinkingly.

For a moment an expression of hope lighted Pam's features, then she sighed. "No such luck, I'm afraid."

"It must be terrible," Robyn said quietly, "to love anyone as much as that."

Pam rose to her feet, stooping to brush the sand from her legs. "How do you know you don't?" she said, and began to walk away towards the house.

Robyn stared after her. What a thing to say! Whatever could she mean? Close on the thought came another – the shame-making conviction that she could very easily feel that way about David. Placed as she was, it was a risk she would have to take! Running down to the water, she struck out with firm strokes, trying with physical activity to dispel the disturbing thoughts Pam's words had evoked.

CHAPTER VI

WITHIN a few days the workmen arrived at the guesthouse. Tall, powerfully built Fijians, they tumbled out of dust-coated trucks and, seemingly impervious to heat and humidity, began without delay to tear down rotting timbers and to rip out inside walls, leaving parts of the building open to sunlight and stars. Scaffolding was erected and before long the air was filled with the sound of hammering and the rasp and buzz of chain saws.

As the days went by she found herself endlessly looking for David, her eyes scanning the fragment of the coast road visible from the house in search of his long red car. But of course he didn't *have* to be here. Why should he? He had already completed the plans for the renovation. Now the actual manual labour was over to other hands, building contractors, plumbing firms, electricians. There was no other reason to draw him back to the Islander. Johnny, angry and resentful, had vanished into the blue and of course David wasn't interested in her. Not in *that* way, the only way that mattered. Except of course as someone to tease, to argue with. She couldn't understand why she missed him so. He wasn't even all that good-looking, only dark and burly and easy to get along with (except when they had one of their frequent arguments).

By the end of the week the new outline was taking definite shape and soon the smell of paint mingled with the resinous tang of freshly-cut timber. Over the paths winding amongst the palms concrete was being poured in an endless stream and on the slope fronting the main entrance a bulldozer was busy churning up sand and earth in preparation for the construction of the turtle-shaped swimming pool.

And still David hadn't come back to the Islander. As day followed day Robyn continued to take the *Katrina* out to the

114

gardens of the reef. It was so easy to manoeuvre the boat nowadays that she couldn't think how she could ever have imagined it to be difficult. Even without a larger craft she could still have arranged for one of the native boys to dive in the water and recover bounty from the deep, but somehow the scheme didn't appeal any longer. Even to herself she refused to admit that it was because David had been adamant on that point and somehow she hesitated to defy him.

The remainder of the time she was free, to wander barefoot over the sands, to swim and sunbathe and dream. Johnny might come to his senses in time and decide to work in with David after all. It would be so wonderful because then she would be free to ... to ... Always at this point her thoughts stopped. She would be caught in a longing piercing in its intensity. If only David would come back! This time things would be different. She wouldn't even mention Johnny's name and spoil everything.

Yet when he did arrive she was taken by surprise. She hadn't seen his car in the driveway and coming up from the beach she suddenly found herself looking up to meet his friendly grin. "How's everything going, Rob?" His tone was quite impersonal.

"Oh ... fine." Swept by confusion, she didn't know what to say. If he was still thinking in terms of their last stormy meeting, and this was the way he wanted it ... A building overseer was approaching along the winding path, and with a hurried "See you," she flung him a smile and went on towards the house. If he wants to see me he can easily find me, she told herself, but he made no immediate effort to seek her out and, piqued and hurt, she took care to keep out of his way.

It was really surprising, she found during the following days, how easy it was to avoid someone if you really put your mind to it. Especially when there was so much movement going on all around her. When for all her efforts to avoid him, her cool nod was met by his smiling greeting, she hurried on, giving him no opportunity to linger.

Looking back it seemed to her now that the shining happiness of their meeting at the native markets, the cruise on the *Olooloo*, might never have been. Forget it, Rob. Better not to let yourself get involved with him. Good thinking, but somehow difficult to put into practice. Had he approached her, asked her to forget their differences, make it "start-again" time once more, she knew she wouldn't have hesitated to meet him half-way, not for one moment! Only he never did. Perhaps he was too busy with his own activities to waste time with a stupid girl with crazy schemes for coral boats. More likely he just ... didn't care. Especially now that he was expecting his "friend" at the Islander, that super-efficient woman who, from what she could gather, was just about everything that she herself wasn't! Trained to a high standard of efficiency in dealing with the public, an expert in all aspects of tourism; confident, poised, inwardly secure. Lovely to look at too, she wouldn't wonder, Robyn mused moodily.

But whatever their private differences she was forced to admit that David deserved his reputation as a leading architect of the South Pacific. Without apparent effort and in spite of lazy island atmosphere he seemed to have a knack of getting things done. Now that the project was nearing completion she could see that he had achieved his objective, that special harmony with the elements of nature. How had he put it? "An involvement with the environment." For viewed from the vantage point of the *Katrina* out at the coral reef, the low thatched roofs and stained timbers in the shelter of the clutered coconut palms fringing the sandy shore blended to form part of the surrounding landscape.

One day on her return from her trip on the glass-bottomed boat she found a letter awaiting her. It was from a large group of travel promoters with headquarters in Suva, commissioning the painting of a special mural featuring facets of Fijian life to be hung in the native-style restaurant of one of a chain of world-class hotels now in the course of construction in the islands of Fiji. In addition she was requested to execute a number of wall hangings in the media of black velvet, preferably native women and child studies.

Robyn couldn't understand why she wasn't more excited over this unexpected stroke of good fortune. She had heard of the Plantation, of course, one of a chain of luxurious hotels now being erected on the opposite coast. To have her pictures on exhibition there must inevitably lead to further commissioned art work of a similar nature. It was wonderful of Johnny to have mentioned her name and thus put the opportunity her way. Why then wasn't she more elated by this sudden success? Somehow all she could think of was David. This would serve to show him that she wasn't utterly without talents, even if her gifts didn't lie in the direction of hostessing for the tourist trade. Then she remembered. At the moment they weren't exactly on speaking terms, she and David, and he wouldn't be the slightest bit interested in her affairs anyway. The thought took the edge from the news. Oh, why did he have to spoil everything for her? she thought illogically.

The letter still in her hand, she made her way along the snowy concrete path leading towards the line of bures with their tattered thatched roofing and peeling paintwork. Soon, she knew, the shabby huts would be demolished, but meantime they made a temporary shelter for the staff, Mrs. Daley and herself while the main building was in the course of renovation. David made visits to the Islander from the big hotel around the point. Did he stay there in order to avoid contact with her? She couldn't tell. She wished she knew the answer.

Lost in her thoughts, she didn't see him approaching her. The next moment she was enmeshed in his brown gaze, where surprise mingled with something else ... something that had the effect of turning her mind into a wild confusion so that she forgot everything but the warm intimacy of his gaze, made her cry "David!" in a delighted way when she should have gone right past him with a couldn't-care-less smile. But it was too late. Her heart was racing and he was smiling, and all at once the blue-skied day was electric, like herself.

"Got some mail, Robyn?"

Ordinary enough words. No reason at all for her to feel

this surge of pure happiness. "Oh yes, yes!" Belatedly she wrenched her gaze away and stared down at the folded paper in her hand. "It's fantastic! The most wonderful news ever! Do you know, I've just been offered a commission for a mural and wall hangings. Guess who it's from!"

"Tell me." He looked almost as delighted as herself.

"The plantation! The big new hotel that's going up on the other coast. I just can't believe I've been so lucky!"

"Not lucky, Rob, talented. You know, you deserve a break. Your work's good and you get just the right touch, a balance between modern stylized forms and the spirit of Fiji itself. Going to make it figures or shells and sea stuff?"

"I haven't decided yet." She was still breathless with happiness. "They've given me a free field for the mural, I thought maybe a seascape, and for the black velvet wall hangings I've got to use native figures, women and children preferred."

"Those child studies you made at the native village," enthusiasm coloured his tone, "you could work from those!"

"That's what I thought too!" At the warmth of his voice all her worries were miraculously magicked away. Oh, it was heaven to have him on her side like this, helping instead of opposing her.

"Congratulations! This calls for a celebration, but for a start, how about a personally conducted tour of inspection?"

He caught her fingers in a warm clasp and they strolled over lush green lawns together, pausing to watch the concrete being poured into the hollowed-out shape at the foot of the slope. In a lull in the din of the mixers, David said, "That was an inspiration of yours, having the pool made turtle-shaped. It's something different from all the others on the island, topical too!" He turned to her with a grin. "All things considered, we make a pretty good team, wouldn't you say?" He was squinting into the sun and she couldn't tell whether or not he was making fun of her. You could never be sure with David. Not that it mattered, of course, yet somehow it did – terribly.

The noise started again and he drew her forward. "Come

on, let's get out of here. It'll be much more interesting in a couple of weeks' time when the blue tiles are all down and the infiltration plant's working. After that, I've got ideas about having the slope terraced ... flowering shrubs dotted about ... what do you think?"

"That would be super! Hibiscus – lots of them!" In her new-found happiness all thought of barbed rejoinders and significant silences fled from her mind.

"Colour?"

"Every shade there is! Pink, red, yellow, orange ... and around the edge of the pool, those purple orchids that grow wild around here. They'd be tall enough to lean over the edge of the water."

"It's as good as done! We'll have them." *We!*

As they moved into the shade of the thatched walkway connecting the main building with the wide patio, David remarked, "I've ordered small tables and chairs for this area. Sun umbrellas for the tables set out on the grass and a food bar running along the back wall."

"Could we have violet-coloured table tops with black wrought-iron chairs?"

"Why not?"

They strolled on past small thatched huts now being painted in gay colours that were dotted amidst surrounding greenery. "You know something, Rob? You've been a terrific help to me with all this."

"Me?"

"But you have! I'll tell you something else too." She could scarcely concentrate on what he was saying for the excitement running from his fingers to her own. "Any architect will tell you that his best work comes from a definite empathy with the client ... harmony of interest. You know?"

Was he having a joke at her expense? She couldn't tell. His tone was non-committal, so why was she trembling? Lamely she heard herself murmur, "I'm not a client – well, not exactly." She added in some confusion, "And we haven't been all that close –"

119

"We could be," he said softly.

She caught her breath. Just what did he mean by that? But a workman came into sight, clearly in search of David and he turned to speak with him. Afterwards they moved past the wide picture windows with their vista of palms and lagoon and as they entered the cool dimness of the low ranch-style building, Robyn said, "Tell me about yourself."

He grinned down at her. "Nothing much to tell."

"I don't believe it. Went to school . . . where?"

"Sleepy little village in Cornwall."

"And then?"

"On to university in London for a course of architecture, and that was about it."

"Oh, come on, you must have done something more than just study —"

"Not for a long time. I was lucky . . . managed to gain a travelling scholarship in Architecture that took me to Germany and further study. After that it was private practice in England, then this trip out to the South Pacific. Not a very interesting account, really."

"It is to me." Or would be, she amended silently, if only he hadn't left out all the important things, such as how it was that he had reached the age of thirty or thereabouts and was still a bachelor. Suddenly she found herself feeling awfully glad that he hadn't married a girl overseas.

"This room at the entrance," he was saying, "is to be the craft shop."

She paused beside him. "I can imagine. Quaint little place with lots of local souvenirs — nice ones that folk can take home with them. Especially light-weight articles for air travellers. Clothing too . . . fun shirts for the men, sulus and saris for the girls, for that island dinner. We must have some of those pretty 'butterfly frocks' with the wide sleeves." She laughed up at him. "Just the thing to get the feminine guests into the exotic South Pacific island atmosphere!"

"You don't mind giving a hand there?"

"I don't mind." Today she didn't care about anything, not

120

even conceding him a point on the matter of assisting with the craft shop.

"It'll mean giving up the coral boat excursions you like so much."

"I know. I've thought of that, but it will be only until Johnny gets back –" swiftly she ran on before he could make any comment, "and Selani's got a boy-friend in the village who would be ideal for the job. They're hoping to get married one of these days and it would help him, and her too."

"Great! That's settled, then. You'll need to get in some stock before the opening date. Could I leave that part of things with you? Maybe you could get on the phone and put an order in to the stores in Suva?"

"No problem." The airy mood persisted.

They moved through the kitchen, now transformed into an attractive work area with long shining stainless steel benches, excellent lighting, a long white electric range and electric mixers and dishwasher.

Eve Daley followed them in, her grey locks still damp from her swim.

"Isn't it *hot* outside! Thank heaven for decent air-conditioning at last! As well as for everything else one could possibly wish for in cooking for a crowd of guests!" She put an experimental finger on the drying paintwork. "I'm glad you're getting in a professional chef, David, now the place has a first-class restaurant. I'll be much happier just looking after the housework and keeping an eye on the maids. Right now I'm having a holiday, a good excuse to take things easy. Would you two care to join me, have coffee?"

"Sorry," David declined the invitation, "but we're on a tour of inspection. Self-contained units coming up! On your way, Robyn!"

They moved into the first apartment where the smell of recent paintwork still lingered. Robyn glanced around her in unconcealed admiration, taking in the harmonious colour scheme in tonings of cream and amber and rich browns. Her gaze moved over the twin day beds with their gay covers, white paintwork, white venetian blinds at the windows. The stained floors were covered with matting. "I had no idea the furnishings had arrived."

"They came late last night. I got the boys to give me a hand to arrange them."

She glanced into a small kitchen with its orange table-top and matching chairs, bamboo-coloured painted cupboards, small refrigerator and electric stove.

In the bathroom the primrose shaded bath and basin were matched by a shower curtain printed in a design of the tiny tropical fish that swarmed in the waters of the reef. It was all fresh and attractive, a delight to the eye.

Back in the lounge room she put out a finger to touch a line of switches on the wall. "For goodness' sake," she marvelled, reading out the printed notices, "dry cleaning, laundry, hairdressing, room service – there'll be a knob to press for baby-sitter wanted next!"

"There is, second to the left."

"You'll need an awful lot of staff to run all these different services –"

"We," he corrected gently. "We'll get them. Why don't you try the end button and see what happens?"

For answer she touched the switch and immediately the soft strains of Fijian music with its haunting cadence fell around them. She turned towards him, smiling, "Or would you rather have –"

"This!" He took a step towards her and at the brilliant intensity of his gaze she felt again that wild sense of excitement. Then, "I thought I'd find you here," said a cool voice from the doorway, and Robyn's dazed glance took in the immaculately dressed girl who stood observing them.

"*Ni sa bula*, welcome to Fiji!" It seemed that nothing could throw David, not even the mocking glance of those lively hazel eyes. Or could it be, Robyn wondered over a stab of pain, that he was genuinely pleased to see Maria, for who else could it be?

"The old dear in the kitchen told me I'd find you up here,

and I didn't see any 'do not disturb' notices around." She had a clear ringing laugh, even when there was nothing to laugh about, the thought flashed through Robyn's confused mind. "And anyway, I thought you'd be glad to see *me*, David, any time at all!"

"Of course. When did you get in?"

"Five minutes or so ago, on the local plane. I would have let you know of the change of plan, but Ann rang me in Sydney to say she was making the trip to Fiji too and I couldn't miss out on the chance of coming with her!" Again that peal of meaningless laughter. "I knew you wouldn't mind how early I turned up!" All at once Robyn felt left out, of no importance – worse, in the way. Maria was running on, she thought angrily, just as though Robyn weren't in the room. Did the other girl in her sophisticated black outfit mistake Robyn for one of the maids? Certainly that was the impression she managed to convey.

At last in a pause in the flow of words David said in his deep quiet tones. "Maria ... Robyn Carlisle, the owner. I told you about her when I rang through to you, remember?"

Just how much had he told the other girl, Robyn wondered, of the true position at the motel?

"Owner!" Light pencilled brows rose in surprise (or was the astonishment simulated? Robyn asked herself.) "Oh yes," the careless tone dismissed her with a word, "you're so *young*, aren't you?" She made it sound like a crime, Robyn thought furiously. "Wasn't there a brother somewhere in the picture?" Her tone implied that a bachelor brother was infinitely more interesting than a freckle-faced girl with sand-encrusted bare brown legs and little to say for herself.

"Is he around?"

"No, he –" All at once Robyn caught the mocking expression in the lively hazel eyes. *She knew.* Someone must have told her about Johnny, and who could that "someone" be but David? It seemed that Maria was deliberately trying to humiliate her. If Maria and David were friends, perhaps even something more than friends, wouldn't that explain the other girl's openly contemptuous attitude towards her? Whatever the reason, she doesn't like me one little bit. Well, that goes for me too!

"He's away just now," David came to her rescue.

"But he'll be back, once we're in business again," Robyn put in quickly.

"Will he? You're his sister, you should know!" Maria smiled her gay assured smile. "I certainly hope you're right, but –" glancing towards her in swift apprehension, Robyn caught the flicker of feline malice in Maria's gaze, "from what I've heard he isn't all that interested in the place. I mean, maybe he's looking for an easier way out of his troubles!"

Robyn swallowed the hot words of denial that choked in her throat. What use to argue the matter? Maria's knowledgeable smile would defeat any excuses she might offer in defence of Johnny's behaviour. David must have told her all the facts of the matter. Robyn's cheeks burned at the thought of the other two discussing the feckless Carlisles, now totally dependent on strangers to rescue them from their financial difficulties.

As she turned aside, an inborn habit of politeness made her say, "Would you care to have a look around first, or would you rather go to your room and freshen up after the trip in the heat?"

"Do I look as if I need to?" Maria turned a laughing flawless face towards her.

Confused, Robyn muttered, "No, no, I didn't mean that."

"I'll forgive you." Maria flashed her brilliant smile. Robyn wondered if the other girl would forgive so easily the moment of intimacy she had interrupted a few minutes previously. Aloud she said, "I'm afraid there are only the old Fiji-type bures ready for living in just now. The new units smell so horribly of new paint. But if you don't mind sleeping in a hut like the rest of us . . . it will be only for a day or two."

"My dear child, I don't mind anything!" But Robyn suspected that the other girl minded very much finding her here with David.

"Oh, Maria'll enjoy going native and sleeping out in a thatched hut, won't you?" He grinned towards her. "The fans are still working in the old bures, so it won't be too much of a change of climate after Switzerland."

"You know me, David, anything for a change!" The provocative smile she sent towards him wasn't exactly the smile of a woman chatting with her dead husband's friend, Robyn mused unhappily. *Unless David was something more than a friend.* Her mind went off at a tangent. If only Maria's appearance weren't so perfect! Short-short fitting black frock, dark stockings, black suede shoes. Cropped curly brown hair, a round face with a quick, bright expression. A laughing voice that seemed to imply so much more than the lightly-spoken words. Not outstandingly pretty by conventional standards, but her air of confidence and vivacity made her attractive – at least David apparently thought so. As to the perfection of the lithe figure, of that there could be no doubt at all.

They moved along the hall together, Maria's heels clattering on the newly-varnished timbers. At the entrance David picked up the two expensive-looking travel bags and Robyn led the way down the winding path towards the line of bures.

"You've been busy here, David," Maria was glancing appreciatively around her. "Looks like you've poured a lot of capital into the project. I hope you can get it back again."

"That's where I'm depending on you, Maria."

She turned to smile into his eyes. "Is that the only reason why you dragged me half way around the world?"

Through a fog of misery that had descended around her Robyn mused that it was a loaded question, but apparently David chose to read no particular significance into the lightly-spoken words. "When I think of what you did with that run-down old chalet up in the Alps –"

"Don't forget how much your interior design helped it along –"

"And that tourist hotel in Austria."

"Oh, I had Keith with me then."

"Remember the Italian chef we had there? Those marvellous dinners he used to put on?"

"Could I ever forget Giorgio?"

Robyn had the impression of a door being slammed against her as the other two went on to talk of a sophisticated world that she would never know.

When they reached the shabby bures, Robyn threw open a door. "I'll get Selani to bring some iced water."

Maria didn't appear to have heard. She was standing quite still looking up at the tattered thatch roofing above her head. "Isn't that rather a fire hazard?"

"Could be, but not to worry," David assured her. "You won't be in here for long –"

"And Mrs. Daley told me we've never yet had a fire at the Islander," Robyn put in.

Still the other girl stood motionless. "Who sleeps next door?"

Robyn was puzzled. "I have the one beside you."

"I hope you don't smoke in bed?"

"Hardly ever."

"I'll know who to blame then if anything happens." At last Maria moved inside, giving a swift glance over the shabby interior. She turned to David. "Isn't there anywhere else?"

"It's safe enough, believe me."

Robyn's bewildered gaze went from one to the other. She couldn't understand this efficient, outgoing young woman allowing a mere possibility of danger to put her into such a state of fear. For it was fear ... there was no mistaking the sharp note of alarm in Maria's tones.

"Look, you'll be all right. I give you my word! You'd loathe that paint smell in the new units. Tell you what, make do with it just for tonight. The other bures are open to the air and by tomorrow you can move in and chance the paint. Right?"

"If *you* say so, David." Her smile as she looked towards him was an arrow piercing Robyn's heart.

"I'm sorry it's not more convenient for you." Robyn's apologies died away. It was Maria's own fault if she had to

126

put up with a certain measure of inconvenience. She had arrived earlier than expected and before her new apartment was in readiness for her.

"I've got oodles of messages for you," Maria turned to David. "Bob's set a new skiing record. I don't think I wrote you about it at the time, but you may have read about it in the papers I sent you."

So they corresponded regularly, these two, Robyn mused. Even though it was Maria who was the stranger, she contrived to make Robyn feel that the other two were a twosome and it was she who was the outsider.

"Won't be long, David," Maria was running on. "I'll just put down my things and then you can show me around the grounds."

"I'll be waiting."

Robyn was conscious of a chill sense of dismissal. Turning away, she murmured, "I'll get along." Probably the other two would be far too absorbed in themselves and news of mutual friends to even notice she had left them.

But she was mistaken, for she had taken only a few steps along the path when David came hurrying after her. "Robyn!" She stood still, hoping ... hoping ... Perhaps everything wasn't going to be spoiled after all. David was planning to leave Maria to her own devices and return to the interrupted tour of inspection. Then she realised that Maria had come out to the terrace and was standing watching – and listening.

"About that black velvet," David said. "You'll need a special type of velvet for the painting. I'll cable the warehouse in Sydney today and get a bolt sent over right away."

She stared up at him dazedly, pushing a long strand of hair back from her face. "Thanks, David."

The last thing of which she was aware was Maria slipping an arm through David's, laughing up into his face, her cropped brown hair very close to his shoulder. "Miss me?"

Robyn didn't wait to hear any more. She was hurrying away towards the shelter of the spreading banana palms, any-

127

where to be out of sight of the other two, away from the hurtful sound of the other girl's assured proprietorial tones.

That evening she decided to skip dining with the others in the newly-remodelled kitchen. She sent a message by Selani to Mrs. Daley saying that she wouldn't be in to dinner. Let David make what he liked of her absence. Not, she reflected bleakly, that he would even notice, now that his "friend" was here with him. But why give him and Maria the satisfaction of knowing that her eyes were swollen with weeping? Fool that she was, to have mistaken his friendly ways for anything more personal. David was pleasant to everyone. He radiated good temper and warmth − it was one of the traits she liked about him. It meant nothing, except in her own stupid imagination. To think she had hoped that he felt something warmer towards her! She must have been crazy to dream up such thoughts. How could she go on living here with the other two always near at hand, for no doubt David would be at the Islander more often now that Maria was here.

She stayed in her bure, restless, fighting the tide of misery that threatened to overwhelm her. Perhaps if she began work on the mural, sketched out a few rough ideas from which to choose a final design. Dropping to the floor, she lay face downwards on the matting, a sketch pad open before her, but the ideas refused to come. Instead of a tropical scene she saw in her mind the faces of a man and a woman, laughing and intimate. Still she persisted, knowing all the time it was useless, until at last she threw down her pencil and moving to the window, stared moodily outside. The soft dark night had fallen and someone was approaching along the winding path lighted by iron stanchions. In the fitful gleam of the blowing flares she caught sight of David and Maria. She threw herself on the bed and must have fallen into a doze, for some time later, turning restlessly on the pillows, she was aware of a man's deep familiar tones, "'Night," and knew that David had seen Maria back to her bure. His footsteps died away as he returned to the main building.

Less inclined now than ever for sleeping, Robyn switched on the bedside light and attempted to concentrate on a novel, but the printed words danced crazily before her eyes. At intervals as if in sympathy with her mood, shafts of lightning played over the room in brilliant illumination. At length she threw down the book and lighting a cigarette, stared unseeingly before her. How to endure being here with David and Maria tomorrow . . . and all the other tomorrows?

At some hour of the night she must have dropped off to sleep, for she found herself struggling back to consciousness, longing to return to oblivion yet pricked by an alertness of something demanding instant attention. Dazedly it came to her then that the room was pervaded by a strange smell. Smoke! Wide awake now, she realised that flames were running up the curtains and licking around the floorboards. The hut was on fire! What had she learned about fire drill? No matter, get to the door! To linger here would mean unconsciousness, followed by death. Gasping and coughing as her lungs filled with smoke, she struggled towards the entrance. Had she locked the door last night? She couldn't remember. At last, after what seemed an age, she wrenched open the door and stumbled blindly out on to the pathway. At the same time a man came running towards her and she all but fell into his arms. David paused only for a moment. His searching glance ran over her. "Are you all right, Rob?"

"I think so. I –"

But with a swiftly spoken, "Call the others! I've got to get to Maria!" he had left her and hurried towards the adjoining hut.

Still in a daze, she ran to the line of bures, flinging open doors, calling loudly, "Fire! Quick! Get out!" In a few moments the occupants of the bures came hurrying out of the openings. Mrs. Daley wearing her long white nightgown, the Fijian boys who slept in the next hut, Selani. The men ran towards the sheds and Robyn guessed they were in search of buckets with which to attack the encroaching flames.

129

Shaking with shock, she watched a cloud of smoke billow from the smouldering thatch of the bure occupied by Maria. It was clear that only the last two huts in the line of bures were on fire although the next one to Robyn's, tinder-dry, was already starting to smoulder. It seemed an endless time since she had seen David kick open the door of Maria's hut. "Don't let him be hurt," she prayed. "Don't let anything happen to him!"

"Come along, Robyn," Mrs. Daley was saying, tugging at her arm, but Robyn shook her head. "Soon."

At that moment a man's figure emerged through the flames of the open doorway. In his arms he carried a small inert figure wrapped in a singed blanket. Robyn caught a glimpse of Maria's deathly-white face as he strode towards her. "Robyn! Come along to the house, quick!"

Obediently, she found herself hurrying along at his side, like a pet dog, to be ordered about, while Maria had to be carried with the utmost tenderness in his arms. As they reached the main building she glanced back where figures were silhouetted against the red blaze as buckets of sea-water were dashed on the flaming bures. Then she followed David as he hurried into the hall and into one of the units.

He laid the inert girl on the bed. "Got any brandy?" he enquired of Mrs. Daley. The older woman nodded. "Get some into her right away, will you? I think she's only overcome with the smoke . . . should come out of it before long."

As Mrs. Daley hurried away, the blanket slipped from Maria's unconscious form, revealing a froth of nylon pyjamas and negligée. Robyn shivered to think of what would have happened to the inflammable fabric had not Maria been rescued from the burning hut.

In a few minutes David came back into the room, his anxious glance moving swiftly to the unconscious figure. Then picking up the brandy he went to kneel at her side and held the glass to her lips.

Maria choked and spluttered, then her half-conscious gaze flickered towards him. "David . . ." All at once she jerked herself to a sitting position, her face alight with terror. "It happened ... the fire ..." The hazel eyes were wide with fear.

"It's all right," David seated himself at her side and took the small white hand in his reassuring clasp. "You're not hurt, Maria, no one is. There's not a thing to worry about."

Her lips were working, out of control. "But there was a fire —"

He ran a smoke-blackened hand over singed hair. " 'Was' is the word! I've just been over to have a look at the bures, or what's left of a couple of them. The boys got the fire under control without too much trouble, even if they did have to depend on hand labour and buckets of sea-water! Not that it would have been any great loss if all those tumbledown shacks had gone up in flames. They're due to be demolished any day now." Was he talking to give Maria reassurance? Robyn wondered. To take that stricken look from her eyes? She could scarcely recognise in this abject, terror-stricken girl the self-possessed young woman of earlier in the day. It was odd, because she would have imagined Maria to have been well able to cope confidently with anything that came her way, even to a fire in her hut on her first night here. Yet she was obviously in a state of shock that appeared out of all pro-portion to the hurt she had sustained. "I never wear nylon underwear," she spoke through chattering teeth, "but last night I forgot." She continued to cling to his hand with a compulsive grip. "Where did it start, the fire?"

"Next door to you, actually."

"I know!" Maria's accusing gaze went to Robyn's face, with freckles standing out against the pallor. "It was *you*," she cried wildly. "It was all your fault! You were smoking in bed! Look at her! " Wildly she swung around to face David. "Still in the clothes she was wearing yesterday! She fell asleep while her cigarette was still alight and set fire the bure!"

Robyn was miserably conscious of her crumpled shift, the singed shreds of the chiffon scarf with which her hair was tied back from her face. For a moment she couldn't remember. Was the table lamp still lighted in the bure when she awoke? She couldn't deny the charge because she wasn't certain herself of what had happened.

"You've got it all wrong, you know." Unexpectedly David came to her rescue. "The boy who came running to tell me about the flames said he'd seen the thatch on the roof catch in a sheet of forked lightning. I beat him back to the bures by about a minute!"

Maria took no notice. "I warned her about that very thing! I told her not to –" To Robyn the other girl appeared to be on the verge of hysteria.

"I'll go and make some tea." She slipped away, meeting Mrs. Daley outside the door, an incongruous figure still wearing her old-fashioned nightwear. The older woman glanced from the tray of teacups in her hand to Robyn. "One of these is for you."

"Thank you, but I'll have it in the kitchen with you and the others."

Robyn dropped down at the table where Selani and the native boys were already gathered, their huge brown eyes wide with excitement as they discussed the events of the night. Presently through the clamour of voices she became aware of David. He was pouring a cup of steaming tea from a massive teapot and sliding it along the table towards her. "Come on, Rob, down that!"

It was a little late, she mused, suddenly weary, for David to be regarding her with that look of solicitude.

"No after-effects?" He was eyeing her intently.

"None at all."

"Too bad about your stuff. The fire made a clean job of everything inside your bure. Was there anything in particular there that you won't be able to replace?"

She raised her heavy glance to his. Only a love affair, David, but I'm not letting on to you about that! Aloud she murmured, "Not really. Some boxes of paints, a couple of sketchbooks, nothing all that important."

"How about those pictures of the island kids you made in the native village that day?"

So he could still spare a thought for details of her small unimportant doings. "It's all right. I lent them to Selani to show to her sister and she hadn't got around to returning them."

"What about gear?"

Robyn shrugged. "Just a few shifts and things, a couple of bikinis. Nothing very expensive." Not like Maria, who would have lost a wardrobe of high-fashion garments. She remembered the soft creamy leather travel bags. Anyway, an experienced traveller like Maria would be certain to be well covered for the value of her personal belongings. Not like herself. There was no insurance against a lost love! She sighed and brought her heavy thoughts back to David's tones.

"I've got to get back to Maria. She's taking all this pretty hard, poor kid."

Kid! Belatedly she remembered that only his prompt intervention tonight had saved her from real danger, possibly even the loss of her life. "Thanks for . . . coming along," she murmured diffidently. Somehow it was awfully hard to concentrate on the words when his gaze was fixed on her downcast face. "It was so late. How did you happen to be still here?"

"Oh, I'd stayed on at the house, working on some plans I was drawing up. I'd just decided to pack it in and call it a day when one of the boys came in shouting that he'd just seen smoke pouring from the roof of your bure."

"Lucky for me!"

"Luckier for Maria."

Of course he must consider her first of all. From now on, she mused bleakly, it would always be this way. Maria, Maria.

"I'm taking her back to Suva for a few days," David was saying. "The Islander isn't quite ready for guests yet and a change of scene might serve to get the whole thing out of her mind. Before she comes back I'll see that the old bures are pulled down. That way, there'll be nothing to remind her of what happened tonight."

Robyn wanted to ask him why it was so important that Maria shouldn't be upset in the slightest degree; why he had to go to so much trouble simply for the sake of a new manageress for the Islander. But of course she wasn't thinking straight tonight, she told herself. Why fool herself? Maria was someone special, a girl for whom he obviously cared a lot.

His voice softened. "You'll be all right, Rob? You've got no bad burns, nothing like that?"

"I told you, I'm fine. I got out just in time, not like Maria —"

"No." His tone was abstracted. "It was bad luck, this happening to her. If only there's no permanent damage . . ."

What could he mean? she thought, mystified. "But she wasn't badly burned, was she?"

"No, no. It's just —" He checked himself, frowning thoughtfully and whatever it was he had been about to say, he changed his mind. "She needs looking after for a few days, that's all."

All! Robyn crushed down the hot words that rose to her lips. She might as well get used to the fact right as from this moment that he could think of no one but Maria. Almost she was glad that they were both leaving in the morning!

CHAPTER VII

"A TELEPHONE call for you, Robyn, from Suva." Mrs. Daley's grey head was thrust around the door of the unit where Robyn had transferred her few personal possessions left undamaged by the fire. Suva! Perhaps it was David! She flew to the telephone, then remembered just in time about Maria and schooled the excitement from her tones.

"Robyn!" In spite of everything her heart gave the familiar lurch at the sound of his voice. "How are you feeling now? No after-effects, shock, nothing like that?"

"No, I'm still disgustingly healthy, but it was nice of you to ring." Once again an inborn courtesy prompted her to say, "How's Maria?"

"Not too bad. Once she's over the shock of it all she'll pick up. You haven't forgotten that date we had to look around for some stock for the new shop, in Suva?"

Forgotten! When she had been looking forward to the outing so eagerly – but of course that was before Maria's arrival. It would have been fun, the wistful thoughts ran through her mind, choosing souvenirs and clothing together. Now she was determined to deal with the buying of the stock herself. If she made a wrong selection at least that would be preferable to being forced to spend the day in the company of David and Maria.

"Call me back," he was saying, "you can get me any time at the Outrigger and I'll come over and pick you up. We'll make it a fairly small order for a start, then see how we make out. Which day –"

"I'll let you know," Robyn said faintly.

"Make it soon! I'll be down before the end of the month. I'm arranging for a *Magiti* – know what that is, Rob?"

"Isn't it an island dinner, dancing –"

"You've got it! Actually it's to mark the official opening

of the Islander. It won't matter if guests have been staying for a week or two before that. I can count on Maria to have everything under control."

No doubt, Robyn agreed waspishly. Apart from her obsession in regard to fire dangers, nothing could ever throw Maria!

"I'm fixing the date as the thirtieth . . ." A pause . . . there was no alteration in his friendly tones, but then was there ever anything to which she could pin him down? "Any chance, would you say, of getting your brother to come along?"

"I'll try." She endeavoured to infuse some certainty into her tones, but deep down she realised he knew that she had no idea of Johnny's whereabouts. He could have returned from a short cruise around the islands in the *Noeline*. If only he would let her know. Lamely she heard herself say, "He promised me he'd be back at the Islander as soon as the place got going again."

"Okay, then. I'll leave that part of the proceedings to you – you're sure you're feeling all right, Robyn?" That was the disadvantage of the telephone, it magnified nuances, betrayed feelings you had scarcely acknowledged yourself, like loving him so much . . .

"Yes, yes, of course I am. See you later, then." Having cut the conversation short, she immediately regretted it. Oh, what was the matter with her that she could never hide anything, even being in love with him, in spite of Maria, in spite of everything. Listlessly she turned away, staring unseeingly out at the swishing banana palms that brushed the patio.

A light tap on the door interrupted her musings. "Was that David on the phone?" Mrs. Daley came to stand at her side. She nodded. "He was just asking how everything was around here."

The older woman sent her a shrewd glance. "Well, I don't think you look all that wonderful. Peaky, that's how you look. You've had a shock, Robyn, and it takes some getting over." (More of a shock than you'll ever know, Mrs. Daley). Robyn

136

wrenched her mind back to the friendly tones. "Why not take a run into Suva? You've still time to catch the bus. You'll need to replace the clothing and stuff you lost last night."

Robyn dragged her heavy thoughts from David — and Maria. "David wants some stock for the craft shop. I'll have to go in one day soon to choose it." No need to explain that she had to force herself to the task for which she had no enthusiasm, not now. "But what about the coral boat if I'm not here?"

"Don't give it a thought! Selani's Lesi will be only too pleased to have the chance to take the tourists out to the reef. He's a reliable type of Fijian, one of the best!' "

"Perhaps I will." Listlessly she reflected that the trip to Suva would be something to do, an activity to take her mind from her own dreary thoughts and the mental pictures of Maria and David, happy together as he escorted his "friend" around the tourist attractions of the city. Actually, she had urgent need to make a visit to Suva in order to replace the clothing she had lost in the fire. Then too she must purchase a new supply of painting materials, oils, sketchpads, pencils. She should be making an immediate start on the newly-commissioned mural. She would, she promised herself, once she got the better of this sense of heartache that left her with no interest in anything, not even the art work that was such a wonderful career opportunity. Trouble was, she didn't want a career. She yearned for all the fulfilment of a once-in-a-lifetime love affair, marriage ... she wanted David. Oh, what was the use? She wrenched her thoughts aside and brought her mind back to Mrs. Daley's kindly tones.

"That's more like it. Do you good to have a change. If you have time why don't you go up to the house? It's right in the town, on the hill overlooking the harbour. The boys are always wanting to meet you," the weather-roughened face broke into a teasing smile, "especially Kevin, that younger son of mine. He'll be around the place, I expect. If you see him tell him from me that he's got to get down to his studies. He's simply got to get a couple of units at least this year at university or I'll want to know the reason why."

"I'll tell him, if I see him." Inwardly, however, she had no intention of visiting the house on the hill in Suva. In her present mood of despair she was in no humour to meet strangers, no matter how friendly.

Forcing herself to concentrate on the matters in hand, she enquired of the older woman the names of stores likely to stock the souvenir and local craft articles she needed for the new shop at the Islander.

"You could probably pick up things a lot cheaper at the market."

"No, I don't want to go there!" Today she was in no frame of mind to be reminded of the day she and David had spent there together.

Mrs. Daley misinterpreted her objection. "It is awfully crowded, and smelly too – all that fish – but there are lots of small stores where you'll be able to find what you want. I'll make out a list, then you won't have to waste time looking for things in the heat."

"Thank you."

"And don't forget, if there's no one at the house, just open the door and make yourself at home."

An hour later, wearing the orange-coloured shift that was the single frock remaining from her scanty wardrobe, Robyn stepped on to the bus that lumbered to a halt in the dusty road at the entrance to the motel. The vehicle took the road that coiled along deserted sun-splashed beaches, before it curved inland to plunge through a riot of tropical trees, bamboo groves, ferns and wild hibiscus bushes. Presently they cut between great hills covered in dense jungle growth and at last turned into a smooth highway. Ahead shadowy blue hills rose beyond the harbour. Small bays swept by, clustered with fishing craft and cruisers. Was one of those white-sailed keelers the *Noeline*? And was Johnny still aboard as one of the passengers on the luxury yacht?

Presently they ran into the busy streets of the city, threading their way between the bluest of seas while cars and taxis and trucks laden with local produce for the nearby open market shot around them. The beauty of it all, the heat-hazy day, the great spreading banyan trees throwing their shade over the colourful street, all underlined Robyn's own heart-ache. Somehow she must pull herself together, think of the tasks ahead, concentrate on souvenir stores, new clothing for herself.

She strolled along the side street where Fijian women, hibiscus blossoms tucked in thick dark hair, mingled with Indian women in their brilliantly coloured silk saris. There was a sprinkling of tourists who had no doubt recently stepped ashore from the great white cruise ship berthed in the harbour nearby.

Pausing at the plate-glass windows of a modern store, she eyed the wealth of treasures on display. China ornaments from leading manufacturers in England, pearl jewellery from the Orient, jade from the East. Then she moved on, passing small Chinese restaurants and native tailors' shops. When she found the stores on her list they proved to be of quite a different variety, dark bazaar-like places crammed with a medley of souvenirs, native handwork and printed cottons. In one she purchased silk saris and lengths of cotton material printed in primitive designs of lizards and sea shells and tropical flowers. In another, she bought fun-shirts for men and boys. A little further along the street was a tiny store stocked with scuffs and sun-hats woven from coconut fibre and decorated with shell ornaments. There were necklaces of shells and seedpods, hula skirts made from dyed fibres – even miniature hula skirts for little girls.

For herself from a European store she selected light woven sandals, gaily-printed T-shirts, cotton shorts, vividly patterned shifts and bikinis, undergarments. To the pile of garments lying on the counter she added a peasant frock with cool white muslin embroidered top and a long dark skirt that would swirl around her ankles. Maybe it would serve to give a lift to her sagging confidence, help her through the evenings that lay ahead.

As she had expected in a city famed as a mecca for artists from all parts of the world, she found no difficulty in replacing her paint losses. The art materials together with her personal purchases she took with her and the grateful storekeepers assured her that the stock for the craft shop would be delivered to the Islander within a few days. That should please David – and Maria – she thought bleakly.

Perhaps this would be a good opportunity to try to get in touch with Johnny. At least she could telephone the home of the girl with whom he now spent so much of his time. Not that she wished to ring Noeline's home, but it was the only way she could think of to contact Johnny, and she did want him to be at the official opening of the motel, if only to prove to David that her faith in her brother was justified after all.

She went into the nearest telephone booth and in some trepidation dialled the house. There was no answer, so she tried the Yacht Club. A polite masculine voice assured her that yes, he knew the girl Robyn was enquiring about. At the moment she was away on the family yacht together with a party of friends and relatives and he wasn't aware of the date they were due back. Was there any message?

"It doesn't matter." With a sinking heart she replaced the receiver in its cradle. At least, she'd *tried*.

She still had the afternoon to fill in before catching the daily bus back to the Coral Coast. She could of course wander up and down the street, inspect more closely the luxuriously appointed stores to which she had given only a cursory glance, explore the small alleyways and places of local interest. But what if she came face to face with those other two in the street? The thought made her change her mind concerning Mrs. Daley's family home. At least it would be somewhere to go, and maybe if she were lucky enough, there would be no one at the house and she could spend the time there alone.

The heat was increasing and her footsteps slowed as she made her way up the steep slope where houses and tall apartment blocks rose amidst vivid greenery, and the air was per-

140

vaded with the perfume of the pink and white frangipani that grew wild on the slopes. Tall orchids raised their velvety lilac heads amongst the grass and hibiscus flowers shone with a translucent brilliance in the hot sunshine.

She found the house without difficulty, a sprawling white bungalow with peeling paintwork and a jumble of rooms obviously added to the original building.

The door bell didn't seem to work. Breathless and hot, she knocked and after a moment felt relieved to hear no sound of footsteps on the other side. At least this would be somewhere where she could get a drink. Even water would be welcome at this moment. She opened the door and went inside, moved down a long hall with doors opening off on either side. At the end she glimpsed painted yellow walls, a sink bench. Robyn went into the room and found herself staring down at a tousle-headed young man who was seated at the worn table, a profusion of textbooks spread out around him.

She couldn't help a smile at sight of his amazed face. The next moment he rose with a grin. A tall thin young man wearing strong glasses and bearing not the slightest resemblance to his mother, if Mrs. Daley was as she supposed his mother.

Robyn was the first to recover. "I'm so sorry, bursting in on you like this —"

He made a movement that sent a towering pile of textbooks spinning to the floor and Robyn bent to help him pick them up. "I did knock, but you couldn't have heard me. I'm Robyn," she stacked a pile of books on the table, "and you must be Kevin."

"Right." He was regarding her with unconcealed delight. "Mum told us that the new owner of the old place had turned up out of the blue. She didn't say the important things, though." His appreciative glance swept over the serious grey eyes, the fall of shining hair. "Or believe me, I'd have been out there ages before this! Mum said you would drop in at the house to see us some time —"

"Well, I've dropped! You haven't a drink of water to spare for a thirsty traveller, have you?"

141

They laughed together, then he hurried towards a cocktail cabinet and she heard the clink of ice.

"You can stay to lunch? I was just going to rustle up something."

"Well ... if you let me help you with it." It was amazing how easy she found it to talk with this stranger, yet with David ... was it because she loved him that she always seemed so stilted and stupid? Oh, why think of David anyway? He wouldn't be wasting time thinking of her, that was for sure!

Kevin was sweeping up armfuls of books and papers and throwing them on a shabby armchair. "There's cold chicken in the fridge, pickles –" He seemed pathetically anxious to please her. "I'll put coffee on to perk, it won't take any time!"

Something about the young boyish face reminded her of Johnny. Or was it Johnny as she had imagined him to be? The brother she knew was a stranger, someone she felt she didn't know at all.

"But what about all your studying?"

"Forget it! I can get back to that any time."

She sent him a teasing glance as she passed him on the way to the fridge. "I've got a message for you from your mother about that –"

"Oh, Mum! She's always yakking on about me going out too much. I keep telling her that I manage better this way, leaving all the swot until the last couple of weeks, then cramming it in night and day until I've got it. Pickles coming up! And cole-slaw. You like cole-slaw?"

She set the cold chicken on the table. "You didn't mention interruptions in your programme, you know."

"You think I *mind!*" He sent her an incredulous, laughing look, as though, Robyn thought, the day was something special to him. David had never treated her like that. Once she had imagined he had felt that way about her, but now she knew it had been just an illusion. He was pleasant and smiling to everyone, it was just his way.

Kevin crossed the room, touched the switch of a record-player and the next moment pop music flooded around them.

"Penny for them?" She jerked herself back to awareness. "Oh, I was just thinking of your mother, and how indispensable she is out at the Islander. All that cooking, and the way she manages the native girls."

"She likes people, that's why, and they like her. She told me on the phone the other day that the old place has had a face-lift and there'll soon be a continental chef in charge of the cooking arrangements."

"She didn't mind?"

"Not a bit. She's quite happy to look after the staff, see that the place is clean and tidy. Any job at the Islander would do her. It would take a bomb to dislodge her, she's so attached to the old place. I guess she's just about part of the scenery by now." He eyed her over the rim of his beaker of coffee. "Say, that fire must have been a shocker. Lucky the place didn't all go up in flames!"

"It was rather, but it didn't matter so much about the old bures. David said they were due to be demolished anyway."

"David? Oh, you mean the architect guy who got the job of drawing up the plans and renovating the old place?"

"That's right." Robyn sipped her coffee, fearful that she might betray her interest in the "architect guy." "Do you know him?"

"No. Heard about him though, who hasn't? He's got a terrific name around Suva. They tell me he's got an international reputation in acoustic design. Mum says the old Islander is going to be changed into one of the show places along the coast. You and your brother must be proud of it."

Nice Mum, not to have told anyone, even her own family, the real circumstances that had necessitated the change. Perhaps even Mrs. Daley was unaware of the true position. Come to think of it, she had never discussed with the older woman any business matters regarding ownership or the matter of loans.

When the meal was over he lighted her cigarette, explained the particular subjects he was studying, then took her to the window and they stood looking out to the busy harbour below.

"Look," he ran a hand through springy waves of fair hair and turned towards her, an appeal in his eyes, "I just hate having to tear myself away, but I promised the crowd I'd meet them down at the wharf. Seems there's an Australian girl arriving here today, someone's sister – or something – and they want to take her out on one of the harbour cruises. Why don't you make the trip with us? It's just a couple of hours on the water with a stop-off at Mosquito Island for a swim."

"Mosquito?"

"Don't worry, it's just a name," he assured her.

"Why not?" She had her newly-purchased bikini with her. Besides, she liked this friendly young man with tousled fair hair and an engaging expression, and the outing would fill in the empty hours that stretched ahead; help to combat the feeling of restlessness that possessed her.

Presently she was leaving the house with Kevin and they took the steep winding path leading down to the main street. As they crossed the road to reach the wharves she could see a motor boat moored close by, a wide craft with decks sheltered from the sun by blue canvas awnings. Flags fluttered from the rigging. A group of young people lined the lower deck and as they neared the cruiser voices and laughter reached them.

Almost immediately Robyn was drawn into the group of students, all much of her own age group. Lighthearted and friendly, they welcomed her, treated her as though they had always known and liked her. So why did she feel apart, have to force herself to counter the banter and teasing remarks that fell around her and the tall young man at her side. Fortunately Kevin proved to be gay and talkative so that no one appeared to notice her lack of response. All you need do, she found, was to keep the silly smile glued to her face and the others would do the rest.

The cruiser cast off the ropes and glided over green depths as she nosed her way amongst the varied craft anchored around them. In the babble of voices, the endless talk of 'varsity affairs, no one troubled to enquire who Robyn was or where she came from. Presently the singing crew took up guitars and handsome island boys provided service with a smile as they carried around trays of cool iced drinks and wedges of sweet cake.

Out on the shimmering waters of the harbour, Robyn was aware of a hypnotic feeling that eased for a time the terrible heartache that descended on her without warning. She supposed she answered rationally, laughed and talked with the others as the boat moved on, for somehow the hour went by, then they were turning course and heading towards a tiny, palm-fringed island. A few minutes later the engines cut and the cruiser glided in to the calm waters of a white sandy beach. Passengers with swimsuits and bikinis swinging from their hands began moving down the gangplank.

Robyn went with the others and soon they were taking a sandy path winding amongst the clusters of coconut palms that led towards the changing huts.

The swim in the water so warm it was unbelievable was refreshing and when she returned with the laughing group she felt a slight easing of the tense misery of the endless day.

The cruiser turned and moved in the direction of the wharves and the crew took up guitars. Soon passengers were dancing on the wide decks and Robyn too got to her feet, performing the familiar movements mechanically.

As they neared the clustered craft in the harbour, voices were raised in a chorus of the latest pop song, and passengers moving in time with the lilting guitars formed a long line. Soon others were joining the moving chain that circled the deck and was winding its way up the stairway. Robyn, her hands resting on the waist of a man ahead, went with the others. Singing with the rest, as the stamping line reached the bows of the upper deck, she felt rather than saw that she was being observed, and raised her heavy gaze to David's glance. He was smiling at her, the warm smile that pierced her with a poignancy she could scarcely bear. The next moment a trill of laughter broke the spell and she met Maria's look of amused recognition. Robyn could imagine exactly what she would be saying to David. "Silly kids!"

145

Then she was out of sight of the two standing by the rail, moving with the others as the chain wound its way around the deck and down the stairway.

As the cruiser moved in at the wharf the laughing group broke up but continued to sing in chorus as they moved up the gangplank. Feverishly Robyn tugged at Kevin's arm. "Let's go, shall we?"

"Good idea, get out before the mob. You're coming back to the house, aren't you?"

"Yes, yes!" All she wanted was to get away quickly, before David and Maria could catch up with her. Not that they might have any such intention, but she would take no risks. She couldn't bear to be with them, not today when she was sick with misery and humiliation. She would be certain to make a fool of herself one way or another. And what if he guessed how she felt about him? Or if Maria did? That cool glance missed little. No, she must escape quickly before they could find her in the crowd.

"What's the rush?" Kevin hurried along at her side as she threaded her way through the groups gathered at the water's edge.

"Nothing. Just a habit I haven't got rid of yet!" She flung a backward glance over her shoulder and found to her relief that the other two were amongst the crowd still milling around the deck.

"Hi, Kevin! Robyn! Wait for us!" They found themselves surrounded by a group of students as they crossed the road and made their way up the steep tree-lined slope leading to the white house above.

Afterwards Robyn could never recall with any clarity the details of the remainder of the afternoon. She retained a confused impression of a big room filled with students, of voices raised above the continuous blaring of the record-player and of Kevin always close at hand. Miraculously he appeared to find her company pleasant enough, so she supposed that the answers she gave to his light banter must have made sense.

She gathered that there was to be a party at someone's flat this evening, but feeling in no mood for festivities, she made an excuse of having to catch the bus back to the Coral Coast. As everyone was aware that to miss the vehicle meant having to stay until the following evening, she managed to get her point across without difficulty.

When the time came to leave the house, a crowd of students insisted on accompanying her to the main street. Before the arrival of the bus, however, someone remembered other friends who must be invited to the evening's entertainment and the group moved away, calling farewells and leaving only Kevin.

As the others moved up the darkening street, he turned to her. "Don't think you're getting away this easily! I'm coming down to the Islander. Can't think why I didn't zip down there before . . . if only I'd known. Will you be around at the weekend?"

"Yes – no – I'm not sure." Robyn was scarcely aware of her reply, her attention caught by a red car bearing down in their direction. Of course Suva would have countless cars of a similar make, but if it were David and Maria . . . What if David, guessing she would be at the bus stop, had come to take her back with them to the Coral Coast? At that moment the car, halted at an intersection by a red traffic light, drew to a stop. In a panic she snatched up her bulging zip bags and moved to the edge of the pavement. The bus was lumbering towards her from another direction. If only it arrived first!

The vehicle had barely paused at the passenger stop before she was leaping aboard. Luckily she was the only person waiting there and the next moment they were moving away. On the pavement Kevin still waited, but she wasn't aware of his hand lifted in a gesture of farewell. She was eyeing the car now speeding down the traffic-lined street. If it was David he was too late to catch her, luckily! The car swung into a side street, but not before she had caught a glimpse of David and Maria. She had escaped a meeting with them tonight, but there would be no avoiding them both at the official opening night at the Islander. One more ordeal she must force herself to endure.

The vehicle turned from the smooth bitumen of the main Suva road and took the rough metal surface of the highway winding around the coast. Ahead lush rain forests were a black mass against the night sky and in her ears was the ceaseless booming of breakers pounding on the coral reef. She leaned back against the seat, tears pricking her eyelids.

She loved him, loved him. No use denying it even to herself. From the first she had been attracted to him, more than attracted, and in some sneaky way her feelings had grown and grown until now he filled her world, her thoughts whether waking or sleeping. And each turn of the wheels was bringing her back to the Islander where before long she would have to meet him, talk and laugh and smile and somehow make him think she didn't care!

CHAPTER VIII

ROBYN was moving along the path towards the house after a dip in the pool when David's red car drew alongside. For a second her heart flipped, then settled again, for it was Maria who was at the wheel. The other girl slowed the car to a stop, leaving the engine running.

"Hi!" She leaned from the window, tossing her gay empty smile towards Robyn. "David was going to run me down here, but something came up, something important that he had to see to, so he lent me the transport."

Looking as perfectly dressed as before, though now she wore a simple Island shift, Maria tossed a curl back from her face. Robyn thought she looked rested, happy. Well, wouldn't anyone? There was no trace of the near-hysterical girl of a few nights previously.

Robyn forced a smile. If that was the way she wanted it, to blithely ignore the events of the night of the fire and act as though no wild allegations had been hurled against her, she would go along with it.

"David sent you a message –" Robyn was aware of the cool, *noticing* glance that flickered over her face, realised too late she was tense, eyes alight with expectancy.

"Oh, nothing personal," Maria said with her mocking smile, "he just wanted me to warn you to get ready for the tourist invasion! He's contacted all the local tourist agencies letting them know the Islander is now in business, so the crowd should be heading this way any day now. Is that what you wanted to hear?"

Robyn tried to force her features into an expression of polite interest. "Yes, of course. I'll come along with you and show you to your unit –"

"Don't trouble." Maria slid the car into gear. "David told me to take whichever one I fancy!" A peal of laughter and the car moved away, leaving Robyn with lips pressed tightly together in angry frustration. To be treated with careless condescension by this stranger, her in her own home – well, it was near enough to her own home! Were it not for certain obligations that kept her at the Islander and her promise to David that she would help in the craft shop ... David; once again the black tide of misery swept over her spirit.

The following day found the newly-completed motel hidden amongst the coconut palms to be crowded with guests. Taxis, buses and private cars continued to draw up at the wide concrete parking area at the rear of the building. There was a babel of varying accents as tourists from Canada, England, America, Australia, moved through the foyer and lingered in the boutique on their way to the native-style restaurant. Throughout the day the tortoise-shaped pool was never empty. Afterwards guests lazed on the springy green grass, their bodies glistened with oil and faces upturned to the blue sky as they sought a hurry-up tan. Others hired the specially thick-soled shoes from a thatched hut near the beach and strolled out at low tide to the coral reef.

The newly-painted *Katrina*, now manned by Selani's handsome boy-friend Lesi, was packed with passengers on every trip and stragglers arriving from the neighbouring hotel around the bay were forced to await a second viewing.

It was all working out perfectly, Robyn thought, just as David had planned it – except for her own wayward heart! If only she could get him out of her mind! As day followed day the longing to see him once more intensified. She found herself endlessly longing, looking for him. She had been so certain he would have come back to the Islander before this, if only to finalise arrangements for the opening night. But he hadn't arrived; why should he? With Maria in charge of everything he could be confident that matters would be in hand for the approaching celebration. Oh no, there wouldn't be the slightest hitch, she mused bleakly. The other two no doubt would be on the telephone daily to make arrangements, *and to keep in touch with each other*. That was the hurt.

150

Would it ever lessen? The pain, the aching longing, the dreary sense of despair? She couldn't forget David's attitude towards her on the night of the fire. If anything were needed to underline the directions in which his feelings lay, it was the curt way in which he had brushed past her, all his thoughts centred on the girl in the adjoining bure.

In the days that followed she had to admit that the other girl was proving herself to be an outstanding asset to anyone engaged in the tourist trade. Now apparently fully recovered from the effects of shock suffered on the night of the fire in the bures, Maria appeared to be on duty both day and night. Trim and neat in her short-short black linen frock, her flashing smile welcomed guests and she was quick to see to their comfort. To add to the pleasure of the holiday she arranged daily launch trips to one of the outlying islands, and for shopping in Suva, short air flights travelling in the little blue and white plane leaving daily from the grassy airstrip over the hill from the main building. It was clear that Maria was careful to sustain as far as possible the unspoiled island atmosphere David had envisaged as one of the main attractions of the new Islander. But of course she would want to please him. Robyn hated herself for the thought. They would work in together, they were two of a kind. It was she who was the outsider, naïve, young, inexperienced. In some indefinable way Maria contrived to remind her of the fact whenever they met, which wasn't often, not if she could help it!

It wasn't difficult, for Maria was fully occupied with her duties in the motel and Robyn herself was busier than ever, something for which she was grateful, she told herself, as she threw herself into selling the local curios and native clothing in the small store. For part of the time she was relieved by Selani and for the rest, apart from swimming in the tepid waters or in the pool and strolling at low tide along the reef, she spent her time with canvas and paints in her own modern unit. She tried to concentrate only on matters of the moment as gradually she fulfilled the art orders for hangings, pictures and murals that had continued to arrive from various new

151

tourist hotels and guesthouses that were springing up in the islands of the Fiji group. Come to think of it, she hadn't yet seen Johnny to thank him for putting the commissioned work her way. She had left a message for him at the Yacht Club in Suva asking him to come to the opening night celebrations at the Islander, but so far she had heard nothing. Surely if he was back in time from his cruise on the luxury yacht with Noeline and her parents he would be sufficiently interested to make an effort to be here for that one night. But she knew the hope was a frail one.

On three occasions Kevin had rung her from Suva inviting her out. He urged her to meet him in the city. They'd take in a dinner, a dance, an island show, anything she'd care to see. Robyn had made excuses why she couldn't go. She had to complete art orders, she was tied to the craft shop. Anything but the truth that she had no heart for anything except staying here waiting and hoping for David's arrival.

On the day of the *magiti* Robyn met Mrs. Daley in the hall. The older woman paused with a bright smile. "Did you ever see such a difference in a place? Every unit full all the time and bookings made for months ahead! They say everyone in Fiji is talking about the success of the Islander. They call it the most attractive place in the islands. And that special continental chef David had brought over . . . those tempting creations of his would be the end of anyone not wanting to put on weight. Have you tried his coconut cream pie?"

Robyn shook her head. She hadn't sampled the sumptuous meals so attractively served in the cool, native-style restaurant, It was difficult enough for her to choke down food at all when all the time she was fighting this sense of heartache. She would be thankful when tonight was over, then David would return to Suva and she wouldn't need to see him again. No, she wasn't glad, she wanted him on any terms, even if meeting him again was only misery and pain. Besides, how could she have forgotten, naturally he would be visiting the place as much as ever, only now it would be Maria whom he came to see!

The older woman echoed her thoughts. "You have to hand it to Maria. She's got everything arranged for the opening to-night. No trouble at all. Nothing seems to put her out and she's a marvellous linguist. Just look at her now! The way she's welcoming in that party from Europe you'd think they were the most important guests ever! She's got a real gift for reception work. David was lucky to get her!"

Lucky to get her. The lightly-spoken words sent a pang through Robyn's heart.

"It's just a pity she doesn't know as much about Island ways as she does about tourism in Europe," Mrs. Daley was saying. "The Fijian girls don't take kindly to being ordered about in that authoritative, do-it-or-else sort of way. She hasn't an idea of how to handle staff out here in the islands. They're like children, trusting and laughing and happy, and they'll do anything for you if you treat them in the right way. Oh well," she murmured philosophically, "give her time and one of these days she'll find out that you get better results with the native staff if you play it friendly, let them work along at their own pace more or less, instead of expecting them to jump every time to your beck and call."

"I suppose so." So there was one aspect of management of which the super-efficient Maria was ignorant. For a moment Selani's wistful face flashed to mind. Involved in her own emotional problems, Robyn had scarcely been aware until this moment that the big dark eyes held a shadow of late. Now she came to think of it Selani didn't dissolve into helpless giggles as often as she used to. How could Maria understand? She knew nothing of life in these unspoilt islands where the lazy beat of island music formed an endless background to sea and sand and wind-tossed palms.

"But give her time," Mrs. Daley said cheerfully. "She'll learn, after she's lost a lot of good faithful helpers. Or maybe David will put her in the picture about the relaxed way of life in the South Pacific . . . that is, if he isn't too wrapped up in her to criticise anything she does."

There it was put into plain words, the truth that she had

tried to explain away, but there was no denying it any more. Robyn fled before her unsteady lips and stricken eyes could give away her anguished feelings. Blindly she went out into the brilliant sunshine, hurrying past the pool where guests lazed in the limpid water or sipped ice-cold drinks at the tables set on the grass beneath giant sun-umbrellas. Everyone appeared happy and carefree, everyone but herself. She took a path leading through the wild tangle of coconut palms David had insisted be left undisturbed when the alterations to the buildings were made. High in the branches a chorus of bird song echoed sweetly on the air and she was conscious of the fragrance of frangipani growing wild along the narrow pathway. There was everything here to make her happy – except David! And then she saw him! For all her resolutions her foolish heart gave that too familiar leap. It was too late to turn back, he had already caught sight of her, and slowly she went forward along the path to meet him. Was his smile really so heart-catching or was it merely her own imagining? Just as all at once the sunshine seemed burnished to a higher gleam, the birdsong a wild carol of sound ... and all because David was coming along the path towards her, his face lighted with the special look he seemed to keep just for her.

"I've been looking for you, Rob! Come along, you're just in time!" Suddenly everything was different, the misery of the past weeks swept away as he caught her hand in his warm clasp and drew her along the path at his side.

She had to hurry to keep up with his long strides. "Where are we going?" she queried.

"You'll see in a minute! Ever heard of the firewalkers of Fiji?"

"Yes, but –"

They emerged from the wild tangle of palms on the wide road leading to the native village. The air was acrid with the smell of smoke and Robyn caught the sound of men's voices, melodious and singing in harmony. The next moment they turned a bend in the track and came in sight of a group of Fijian men who were busily hurling great logs on to the

154

flames curling over the huge stones that littered an old pit in the clearing beneath the trees. As a heap of brushwood was thrown over the stones, the flames crackled and leaped high and David drew her back from the intense heat. "You haven't seen the performance yet, have you?"

His touch, his smile, the warm tones of his voice were doing things to her composure. Her mouth said, "I've read about them, and Johnny told me that they'd even performed the ceremony here once or twice, ages ago, when Dad had the place." Her mind was saying, How can he look at me like that, in that deep soft *loving* way, as though he's missed me as much as I've missed him, when all the time . . .

"It's really something! The firewalkers come from Beqa, as far as I know the only island in the world where the ritual's known. You can see Beqa from here . . . there it is, that tiny smudge on the horizon . . ." An arm thrown lightly around her shoulders, he gestured towards a small blur on the shimmering blue of the ocean.

It was no use. His nearness was working its way under her defences. Unsteadily she murmured, "Isn't it something to do with the fire god?"

His gaze was on the men throwing a big log on the leaping flames. "That's right. The legend runs that two priests on the island have handed on to the natives there the power to withstand heat from the fire god. The warriors prepare beforehand for firewalking on white-hot stones, and so long as the particular conditions are kept to, the embers won't worry them. They simply won't feel pain or any heat!"

"Conditions?"

"That means fourteen days' preparation for the special ones. No coconuts to be eaten, no contacts with women. I was darn lucky to have managed to persuade them to come here tonight. Usually the ritual only takes place on their own island and then only once a year. Believe me, Rob, it's a spectacle you'll never forget! They say some devotees undertake to walk the fire in order for the goddess Kali to cure illness in themselves or their loved ones. They believe their immunity

155

to fire was given them by an ancestor who spared the life of a spirit-god he caught while fishing for eels."

"It's incredible!"

"Wait till you see it happen!" He had forgotten to take his arm from around her shoulders.

She was silent, content to be here with him in the filtered sunshine slanting through the breadfruit trees. For a few fleeting magical moments she forgot about Maria and everything else in the sheer pulsing excitement of being with him once again. Then she remembered and quickly, feverishly, began to talk of other things. Her purchases in the stores in Suva, the extra stock needed for the craft shop, the sudden influx of guests. But all the time she knew there was something that must be said. At last she gathered herself as for a great effort, said, "David, about Johnny –"

She caught the imperceptible tightening of the mobile mouth and back to her old uncertain self, heard her uneven tones rushing on. "I tried to get in touch with him to ask him to come to the opening tonight, but I couldn't contact him. I rang the Yacht Club when I was in Suva, but he was away at sea and they didn't know when he'd be back. I left a message there for him, but ... I just couldn't get him," she finished lamely.

"I didn't expect you would."

She shrugged his arm away. "What do you mean?"

"You know what I mean, Rob. Why not face up to things, stop kidding yourself? He's no intention of ever coming back here, not unless he can walk in with a lot of money to back himself up. As to returning here and working for a salary – no, you won't see brother Johnny back at the Islander, unless I miss my guess!"

"You don't know him –"

"Do you?"

He was pleasant, as always. Was it the thought of Maria that drove her on to persist in this inane argument, made her say bitterly, "You never did trust him, did you?"

"What's got into you, Rob?" He reached out to put a hand

156

over her own. "He doesn't matter."

His touch was making her tremble inside. "He does, to me."

But he chose to ignore the low murmur. "Forget about him, he's not worth the worry. Look," his eyes were on the chanting natives as they threw armfuls of brushwood on the flames, "I want to be around when you see the ceremony tonight. I've arranged for the firewalkers to come over from Beqa by outrigger in time to perform the ceremony after the island dinner. Chances are I'll be caught up with the crowd up till then, but I'll be here with you by the pit to watch the firewalkers. Right?"

An impulse she couldn't control forced the words. "I thought . . . Maria . . ."

"Maria won't be seeing this particular show." The light pleasant tones were all at once stern and unyielding. His tone deepened. "It's better for her to keep away. I made her promise me she'd give it a miss."

What could he possibly mean? Could it be that Maria could not be spared from important duties on this particular night and he wanted Robyn with him as a stand-in, a temporary fill-in when for some reason she couldn't understand, he couldn't be with Maria at the enactment of the exotic ceremony? She didn't know who she hated most at this moment – David, who was making a convenience of her, or her traitorous self, for feeling so wildly happy at the thought of being with him again, after all these days of absence!

After that it didn't matter that groups of guests came strolling towards the singing Fijians and soon David was engaged in explaining to them the significance of the blue smoke weaving among the palms overhead. It was enough just to watch him unobserved, to take in the face she loved . . . fool that she was!

That afternoon she was glad of the guests crowded in at the entrance of the gift store. The eager hands thrust towards her helped to make her forget . . . other things. A charming Canadian woman asked her advice in the matter of a choice in the long gaily printed sulu she intended buying to wear at the island dinner tonight. Should she settle for the brown tortoise design or the one printed in green palm trees? Robyn, wrenching her mind from her own problems, was in favour of the palms. She also suggested a matching lei of brilliant blossoms that Selani and the other Fijian girls on the staff had made in preparation of the special island night. An elderly man with a sheepish grin made a purchase of a fun-shirt patterned in dancing dusky maidens, a shy young Fijian girl bought a tortoiseshell hair clasp, a business man selected a miniature model of a carved outrigger canoe to take back with him to his home in the States.

It wasn't until later when Selani arrived to relieve her at the counter that Robyn realised she had made no preparation in the way of special clothing for the evening ahead. She supposed she should make an effort to match the festive occasion in spite of her own feelings. She sighed. Just one more thing she owed to David. Maybe one of the long sulus the Fijian girls wore to such advantage would help her to look like everyone else at the *makiti* tonight, gay and island-orientated and carefree, no matter how she felt deep down.

In a temporary lull of customers Selani smiled down from her greater height. "What are you going to wear to the *makiti*, Miss Carlisle?" she asked shyly.

Robyn raised her heavy glance to the great dark eyes. "I haven't thought. Would you care to help me choose something?"

Selani's broad face broke into a teeth-revealing smile. "I know. This one for you – the butterfly frock." Turning towards the stand with its cluster of vividly patterned cotton fabrics, she extended towards Robyn a short frock.

"I'll slip it on." Robyn took it into the diminutive fitting room still littered with the piles of cardboard cartons she never seemed to find time to sort out and slipped the frock over her head.

In the mirror her face stared back at her with drooping lips and shadowed eyes. She would have to do better than this.

"So lovely!" Behind her Selani's approving glance eased

for a moment the sense of heartache. Robyn lifted her arms and the wide butterfly sleeves fell about her. The white-and-tan patterning of the cool fresh cotton accentuated the translucent apricot of her skin.

"Wait!" Selani slipped away to the big refrigerator in another room, returning with a lei of creamy frangipani. She slipped the flowers over Robyn's shoulders and at once the perfume rose around her, heady and evocative, taking her back to David . . . a deserted beach . . . his kiss . . . a flower lei she had tried to keep alive long after the blossoms had lost their freshness. Just as she was now trying to keep alive a fleeting lost love. Roughly she lifted the flower circle from around her neck. "Put it back, Selani." Then seeing the girl's face fall, she added, "Don't worry, I'll come and get it again later."

"What do you think of this, Robyn?" Maria had entered the room, a length of glittering spangled silk falling from her hands. In a few expert twists she had draped the flame-coloured material around her shoulders and moved to the mirror to study the effect.

Even in a sarong, Robyn thought uncharitably, Maria appeared as though the material were specially woven with her in mind. Aloud she murmured reluctantly, "It suits you." But she knew the other girl wasn't really interested in her opinion. With Maria's undoubted confidence in her powers of attraction, her near-perfect figure, she had no need of anyone else to tell her how well the bright silk with its silver embroidery complemented her appearance.

Robyn made her escape, snatching up the cotton butterfly frock that all at once seemed childish and cheap and ordinary.

The sun had set in a flaming ball over the horizon when a native boy blowing a conch shell gave the signal for young Fijians to light the torches throughout the grounds. From the window of her unit, Robyn watched as guests sauntered towards long trestle tables set out on the grass. The women wore vividly printed shifts and sarongs, bought for the occasion, woven scuffs on their feet, a hibiscus blossom in their hair or a flower lei swinging around their shoulders. The men had twisted lengths of printed material around their waists, some wore a blossom behind an ear, and all were in holiday mood. And David ... from the shelter of the darkening room she saw him move across the shadowed lawns. Casually elegant in putty-coloured shorts, cream silk shirt, a bright cravat, he reached the tables, splashed at intervals with great mounds of hibiscus blossoms. He stood still surveying the guests milling around and obviously searching for someone. Maria, probably, she mused bitterly. It was unlikely that he would notice or even care particularly whether or not she herself was there.

At last when she could delay no longer she moved along the flare-lighted path, a tall girl with long fair hair lifting on her shoulders in the breeze that was blowing the wide wings of the butterfly sleeves of her frock back from her bare arms.

"Robyn! I've been looking all over for you!" Kevin was beside her, his boyish face alight with pleasure. "I was just coming up to the house to ask Mum where you were –" He stopped short, aware of her expression of bewilderment. "Don't tell me you weren't expecting me tonight?"

"Oh yes, I was!" She gathered her wits together. How could she have forgotten their conversation on the telephone only last evening?

He led her towards a table where a party of air crew and hostesses were already seated. Robyn's swift glance raked the group, but neither Pam nor Bruce, the flight-engineer whom she had met on the occasion of her first island dinner, were amongst the party. How could she expect to see Pam here? What would be the use when Johnny had shown her only too plainly that he wanted to finish any emotional ties between them? Pam and Johnny, herself and David. Oh, why was everything so wrong?

She realised Kevin was touching her arm. "Any special seat?" She shook her head, scarcely realising what he was saying as her eyes searched the shadows. Then she caught sight of David as he strolled into the fitful light of the flares, a radiant glittering Maria at his side. At once his glance singled Robyn from the crowd and the other two came towards her. David drew her to his feet. "Just a word to mark the opening of the new motel, folks. First of all I'd like to introduce you all to the owner, Miss Robyn Carlisle!"

Shyly Robyn acknowledged the applause of the onlookers, then David was drawing Maria forward, saying how fortunate was the new Pacific Islander Motel in having obtained her services. In his easy effortless way he went on to say he hoped everyone would enjoy the evening of feasting and dancing, Fijian-style. There was too a special performance to be held tonight, perhaps the strangest and most mysterious ceremony of the islands. Tonight the firewalkers were arriving by outrigger canoes from their island of Beqa to give a performance of the ancient ritual in the old pits a short distance away. Meantime, he was pleased to begin proceedings with the traditional drink of welcome. At that moment the pounding beat of a lali drum cut across the booming of the surf as flower-bedecked Islanders came out of the shadows to place on the tables great wooden bowls filled with Yaqona.

David passed Robyn a glass of the liquid and as their eyes met she wrenched her glance away, tried to smile. "Would you mind if I went back to my place at the end of the table?"

"I'll take you." Almost he appeared to be disappointed, but that was absurd. Why should he mind, when he had Maria at his side? There was, however, no doubt about Kevin's delight on finding her seated once more beside him.

When the welcoming ceremony was over, bowls of steaming island delicacies were carried in – prawns in coconut cream, baked dalo, rourou and Indian curries. They were followed by mounds of tropical fruit, paw-paw, passion fruit, mangoes, bananas. Robyn nibbled a wedge of freshly sliced pineapple and tried to concentrate on what her companion was saying, but in spite of herself her gaze strayed back to David and Maria at the adjoining table.

As the island dinner drew to a close, the idle strumming of

161

guitars quickened and out of the darkness filed a group of Fijian dancers. Their flying skirts of dyed coconut fibre glowed in the flickering lights of flaring torches as men and girls moved in time with the infectious rhythm.

When they fell back, drums beat out a wild tattoo and the next moment tall stately Fijian warriors leaped and chanted, raising their pointed spears in the wild stamping of a native war dance.

Then as the ferocious movements came to an end, guitars once more took up their lazy rhythm and gradually diners moved from the tables to join the swaying Fijian dancers under a canopy of stars.

Thankfully Robyn got to her feet and went with Kevin. She had no wish that David should approach her in a duty-dance. Let him dance with his Maria, she thought angrily. She'd get over this ... this madness, of course she would! All she needed was a little time – and a chance to escape from his nearness. She forced herself to smile and chat, anything to prove to him how happy and carefree she was with her tall young escort.

One of the members of the party of air crew was her next partner and she took the opportunity of asking the air pilot if he knew Pam, as they moved over the dry grass. Was the other girl still on the Fiji route?

"Not for much longer," he told her. At the end of the month she was changing over to the London–Singapore air route. He didn't know why she had applied for a transfer. She'd seemed quite taken up with Fiji for a time, then all of a sudden she never wanted to see the place again! According to the grapevine she'd got tangled up with some guy in the islands. Shrugging his shoulders, he grinned towards Robyn. "You know how it is, or do you? Pacific moon ... soft warm nights ... only sometimes it doesn't last."

Robyn felt a sharp disappointment that she wouldn't be seeing the other girl again. Pam was someone she would have liked very much to have as a friend, a real friend. Now all such thoughts were out of the question. If only Johnny – At

162

that moment she caught sight of him. At least, someone who looked like Johnny was emerging from a short cut through the palms. Then he paused in the shadows and all but obscured by growing bushes, she realised that a slight figure stood beside him. He'd come after all, and brought Noeline with him! With a murmured excuse to her partner, Robyn fled, hurrying over the grass towards the two on the edge of the darkness.

When she reached the other two, excitement coloured her tones. "I knew you'd get here if you could! Did you get my message? I left it with the Yacht Club, but they told me you were away on a cruise and they didn't know when you'd be back. How did you come? How long can you stay –?"

"Hey, hold it!" Johnny stemmed the eager flow. "We just called in to see you, actually –"

"Oh, but you must stay. Look, there's dancing . . . soon the firewalkers are coming. You remember the old pits? They're still here, and David –" She broke off abruptly.

"Would just love to see me? Was that what you were going to say? Well, don't trouble yourself. He's got no time for me, never has had, and I feel the same way about him. I don't have to spell it out, do I? Tell you what – I'll have some definite news for him in a fortnight's time. It won't hurt him any to wait that long. That's an offer, Rob, just two weeks and I'll let him in my plans – definitely. Is that good enough for you?"

She said very low, "He's waited a long time already for you to turn up. You said when the place was in working order you'd be –"

"Hey, whose side are you on? Do you know what I think, Rob? I think you're way over in the enemy camp! All this concern for Kinnear. He can look after himself, believe me, and if you'll take a little brotherly advice, I'd say to keep well clear of him." She caught the teasing note in his voice. "I'm not too late, am I? Don't tell me you're just like all the others? You've fallen for that easy charm of his?"

All the others? Swiftly she jerked herself back to some sort

163

of composure. "Don't be stupid, Johnny! It's just that –"

"Just that you're the world's worst worrier! Well, let it go at that. You think so, Noeline?"

Robyn glancing towards the other girl, caught her nod, the secret smile playing around the thin lips. They were both against her. Suddenly she knew it was hopeless trying to persuade Johnny to accept his responsibilities. Perhaps he was even coming around to her way of thinking in some strange odd way of his own. She had a suspicion the other two were planning to put into action some arrangement in connection with the motel. If only it wasn't the obvious solution that she was trying to thrust to the back of her mind.

"We've gotta get weaving," Johnny was saying. "Just called in to ask you to pass on the word to Kinnear to hold his horses – and to give you an invitation."

"To what?"

It was Noeline who answered, and Robyn found herself wondering at the note of suppressed excitement in the light tones. "It's Mum and Dad, they're putting on a party for me at the hotel next Saturday week. Just a little family celebration at the Lodge in Suva. Think you could come along, and bring David Kinnear too? Dad's thinking of getting into the land promotion game," she ran on before Robyn could answer. "He's ever so keen to meet the architect who's in charge of all the big jobs around here ... might be able to put some work his way."

"Thank you. I'll come if I can."

"And you'll bring Kinnear?" Johnny appeared strangely insistent on the point. He was tapping a sandalled foot impatiently.

"I'll ask him. That's the best I can do." Imagine David escorting her to a function at Johnny's request!

"Good girl," Johnny sounded relieved, "I knew I could leave it to you!"

She raised perplexed eyes. "It can't be all that important his coming ... or me? Why do you want him?"

"I told you, I'm letting him in on my plans for the future.

164

It's what you wanted, isn't it? Besides —"

"You'd be surprised," Noeline cut in lightly. "Anyway, why don't you come along and find out for yourself? Come on, Johnny, the gang will be wondering where we've got to. We've got to get back." She linked a hand in his, threw a smile back over a thin shoulder that landed somewhere in Robyn's direction. "See you at the Lodge!"

"Wait! Wait!" Robyn ran into the shadows of the palms, clutching at Johnny's bare brown arm. But as he swung around she knew it was hopeless. It was useless pleading with him to stay. Instead she found herself saying, "It was very good of you to put all that art work my way. The contacts have led to all sorts of other orders —"

"What art work?" His voice held a puzzled note.

"You know, the commission from the big hotels for the painted murals and hangings. I've really made a start now —"

"I don't get it. What the devil are you talking about?"

"It wasn't you, then? You didn't tell them . . . about me . . ." she faltered.

"I only wish I had, but I'm not guilty this time! Maybe it's your friend Kinnear. I told you he was a deep one —"

"Oh *no!*"

"Come on, Johnny," Noeline urged, "we're late as it is!"

"Coming, honey. 'Bye, Rob, see you at the Lodge!"

"And don't forget to bring David Kinnear with you," Noeline added.

"Goodbye!" Robyn turned thoughtfully away and moved back towards the torchlighted lawns. She was still unable to take in what she had learned. Johnny was right, David was a deep one. But why had he done such a thing? He had nothing to gain by furthering her career. She simply couldn't understand him, but one thing she did know. She would have to thank him and it would take every bit of her courage to do it.

"That wasn't Johnny, was it?"

David stood at her side looking down at her and almost she made the mistake of letting him see the intense happiness

165

he roused in her just by being there. "It was, but he's gone. He was with Noeline and they were in too much of a hurry to stay. He left a message for me to give you –"

His rueful grin was disturbingly correct. "He's not coming back to work for a while?"

"He said he'd let you know something definite about his plans in two weeks' time," she said stiffly. She hadn't intended telling him about the invitation. What was the use, he wouldn't be interested. But all at once she changed her mind, threw it over to fate. "He and Noeline, they want you and me too, to come to a party at the Lodge, in Suva, on Saturday week. Her family are putting it on. I wasn't going to bother telling you –"

"Why not, Rob?" His voice was very gentle. "Don't you like parties?"

"It's not that, but –"

"Me, then?"

Oh, he knew just how to confuse her so that she couldn't think straight about anything ... except his nearness. "You know it wasn't that. I just thought you wouldn't be interested –"

"That's where you're wrong, Rob. I take it you want to go – so we'll go together."

"But what about Maria?" The words were out before she could stop them and at his cool enquiring glance she would have given a lot to recall them.

"I got the idea from what you said," he was as pleasant, as unconcerned as ever, "that the invitation was only for the two of us?"

She nodded.

"Well then ..."

"I didn't think you'd want –"

"I want a lot of things Rob ... like dancing with you ... have you ever danced under the stars?"

He was pulling her along with his warm grasp, fingers linked, and a few moments later they were a part of the rhythmic colourful group moving on the green grass to the haunt-

166

ing music of the throbbing guitars. A cool breeze from the sea sent the palm trees whispering and stirred the greenery surrounding the blowing flares. It was all heady, intoxicating. It would be so easy to allow herself to forget Maria, dancing not far away with one of the guests, her lips curved in laughter. Why not? She had everything in the world she wanted, including David.

Moving in rhythm, Robyn summoned all her composure. "I just wanted to say *vinaka* ... isn't that the word for 'thanks'?"

"That's the word, Rob, but you'll have to interpret the meaning."

"About the orders for pictures," if she kept moving she needn't glance directly into his face, "I thought it was Johnny who'd recommended me to the hotel people, and all the time it was you!"

"That's right. Anything wrong with that?"

"No, no, only I wish you'd told me at the time. Why didn't you?"

"You know why, Rob."

"But I don't." She raised her glance. The way he was regarding her started the trembling inside her.

"Just that you weren't too crazy about me at the time. I got the idea you mightn't have done anything about it if you'd known I was behind it."

"But afterwards?"

"I was saving it."

"*Saving it?*"

"Uh-huh. Special occasion ..." the easy smile.

"I don't know whenever that would be," she heard herself say, inanely, childishly. He was still looking at her in that unfathomable way. "Anyway," she murmured, "it doesn't matter now, does it?"

Before he could answer Maria came hurrying towards them across the grass. "David, the firewalkers are here. They're waiting under the trees by the pit until you're ready for them

167

to start the performance." She ignored Robyn. It was a way of Maria's, and Robyn could never decide whether or not it was deliberate.

"Right, we're ready now! I'll go and have a word with the firewalkers. You get the crowd moving, will you, Maria? Sorry to have to rush away, Rob." He turned and vanished into a pool of darkness along the narrow track. If only, Robyn thought with a sigh, Maria hadn't happened along at that moment. Or had the interruption been entirely accidental? She would never know.

She had entirely forgotten Kevin until suddenly he was at her side. "Come on, Robyn, you're just in time for the firewalkers. Ever seen the performance?"

"No." Together they joined in the crowd moving into the shadows of a narrow pathway. She was relieved when a party of students came hurrying towards Kevin. Now she could be alone with her thoughts. It was David who was responsible for her success in the art world here in Fiji. She still couldn't believe it.

At the end of the track they turned into an old road where flares threw their fitful beams over the stony surface. Overgrown palms along each side of the road tossed in the trade winds, brushing the faces of the laughing, chattering groups who were moving towards the pits. When they came in sight of the glowing embers Kevin was surrounded by the student group and Robyn found herself for the moment alone. All at once a quiver ran along her nerves. Even before he spoke she was aware of him, that was the extent to which David filled her thoughts.

"Now they're preparing for the ones from Beqa." His voice was matter-of-fact and over the tumult of her heart Robyn was aware of colourful figures illuminated in the glow of the fires. A shower of sparks flew upwards as with long vines and sticks the natives raked away the glowing logs, leaving exposed smooth surfaces of flat stones heated to a white heat.

Then out of the darkness, shouting and chanting, came the

Fijian warriors in their bright skirts and swinging leis, muscular dark legs garlanded with beads and flowers.

"If you're a disbeliever, just take a look at their feet after the ceremony," David spoke beside her. "You won't see a burn or a blister." He was very close, his voice in her ear.

"It's incredible!" His nearness was making her pulses leap, filling her with a subtle excitement that had nothing to do with the ancient ritual.

As the party of firewalkers made their purposeful way towards the edge of the pits, Robyn found she was holding her breath. "David, they can't! They'll be burned to death!"

"They won't, you know. Don't ask me how it's done. Just watch and you'll see for yourself. You'll be seeing something not many Europeans have seen. Not many folk have seen the ancient ritual, and those who do experience a spectacle they never forget."

Fascinated, awed, unable to look away, Robyn watched as with no apparent effort a man strode over the white-hot stones. He was followed by others, walking singly and in pairs.

The last man in the line of Fijian firewalkers was almost over the glowing stones when Robyn realised there was a sudden movement amongst the crowd watching on the opposite side of the pit. As the crowd parted she caught David's quick exclamation. "It's Maria! I told her not to come! I was afraid this would happen!" He hurried towards the group on the opposite side of the glowing stones. Someone shone a torch and in the beam of light Robyn saw him lift the inert girl from the ground, then the two disappeared in the darkness.

The ceremony over, the men who had trodden the white-hot stones dropped down to the scorched grass at the edge of the firelight. Cheerfully they raised for inspection the soles of feet quite unharmed and apparently unaffected by heat or burning. Other Fijians were chanting and singing as they tossed leaves and branches over the glowing stones, then covered them with sand.

"Hard to believe your eyes, isn't it?" Robyn became aware

of Kevin's voice. He must have been in the jostling crowd close by her all the time, but, absorbed in the spectacle, and David, she hadn't realised he was there.

"Oh yes, it was worth coming to see!" They were turning away, moving with the groups strolling along the metalled roadway, in the direction of the main building. But already Robyn had forgotten the awe-inspiring spectacle, for something else tugged at her mind. Why had David endeavoured to keep Maria away from the ceremony of the firewalkers, and why had she dropped in a dead faint at the sight of the spectacle? Maria, who appeared to be the most confident of women, not one to collapse at sight of a native ritual, however awesome. She couldn't understand it. All she knew was that whether intentionally or otherwise somehow the other girl appeared to have an unhappy knack of ruining the rare moments Robyn had alone with David. In one way or another Maria always succeeded in drawing his attention away from Robyn and capturing it for herself. Or was she once again being uncharitable towards the other girl?

She couldn't understand Maria any more than she could fathom the reason why David had been instantly agreeable to accept an invitation to a celebration given by Noeline's parents. It was all quite beyond her. All she knew was that she was tired of being used by him as a convenient substitute for someone he *really* loved. Next time she would be stronger, she wouldn't allow herself to fall a victim to the stirring of her pulses – or the sense of his nearness that got under all her defences.

CHAPTER IX

SHE had no need to concern herself over "next time", however, Robyn told herself as the days passed and David did not
return to the Islander. On three occasions she had overheard
Maria ordering a taxi to take her to Suva and Robyn couldn't
help the tide of jealousy that flooded her. For why would an
efficient manageress leave the motel except for something, or
rather someone, very important to her? More important even
than her work here. But of course you would rather die than
enquire as to what business drew the other girl on the long
drive to Suva and back. Anyway, it was plain enough for anyone to see!

On the Saturday morning Robyn awoke with a niggling
sense that the date was somehow meaningful. Then it came
back to her. This was the night on which Noeline's parents
were giving a party for their daughter at their hotel in Suva.
"Don't be late," Johnny had said, and she had promised to
be there without fail, and ask David to accompany her. Well,
she had done what Johnny had asked her and David had ac-
cepted the invitation. That was almost two weeks ago and no
doubt the matter had long since faded from his mind. An
unimportant "forgettable" date with a girl in whom he wasn't
particularly interested . . . now.

A dark cloud of misery engulfed her spirit so that even the
golden sunshine outside meant nothing. She would be thankful when it came time for her to relieve Selani at the gift shop
this afternoon. The crowd of customers might prevent her
from eternally thinking of David. Seeing she had promised
Johnny she would attend the function tonight she would go
to Suva, although she failed to understand why her attendance
at the party should be of the slightest importance to either her
brother or Noeline, unless – why not face it – tonight's function was planned for the purpose of announcing an approach-
171

ing marriage? If that were so then Johnny would have no further need to concern himself with making a living from his island property. Married to a wealthy girl he would no doubt spend his time cruising the south seas in a luxury yacht. Why did she feel this cold touch of apprehension? Was it because she had a suspicion that there was no depth of feeling between the other two? How different had it been Pam and Johnny who were joining their lives. There would be something real there, something worthwhile, but Noeline ... The other girl's secretive smile returned to mind. Johnny would be making the mistake of his life. A high price to pay for the salving of hurt pride and a chance to even a score against David Kinnear.

Robyn sighed. One thing was certain. She would have to take herself to the function, for she hadn't seen David since the night of the ceremony of the firewalkers. The hours dragged slowly by until at last it was necessary for her to relieve Selani in the gift shop.

When she arrived there, however, she was surprised to find that guests were clustered around the closed door. Evidently Selani had left the store earlier than usual. With a quick glance around Robyn went inside. At the same moment Maria came hurrying towards her, an unaccustomed flush staining her cheekbones. "Oh, Robyn, I was just coming to get you. Selani's gone."

Robyn stared at her in bewilderment. "Gone where?"

Maria shrugged. "Why ask me? Home, I suppose."

"But didn't she leave any message?"

"No." Customers were lining the counter and Robyn said no more, but something evasive in the other girl's glance pricked at her mind. Maria knew more of Selani's strange conduct than she had let on, Robyn was sure of it. At last when guests had made their purchases and drifted away, some to the units, others to stroll along the beach, Robyn approached Maria.

The manageress was seated at a desk in the reception room. "Maria, are you quite sure Selani didn't leave a note for me?"

The other girl's gaze was hostile. "Don't you believe me?"

"Oh yes, of course I do. I just thought you mightn't have seen it." As always, Robyn felt herself flurried under the battery of that cool compelling stare. "It's not like her to run off like that. Anything could have happened. Could be she's been taken ill –"

"You can save your sympathy. She's not ill."

A thought flashed into Robyn's mind. She stared down at Maria accusingly. "You didn't tell her to go?"

Black linen-clad shoulders lifted in a disdainful shrug. "It was entirely her own fault. She was insolent. I told her that maybe she could come back here when she's learned how to behave. Maybe."

"Selani insolent? She couldn't be! You must have misunderstood her. Her English isn't the best and sometimes she doesn't understand what you're saying, she makes mistakes –"

"She understood all right. It's time she got it into her head that if she works for me she'll do as she's told and be quick about it! All that 'tomorrow will do' stuff of the islands is all very well, but when it comes to the staff, I won't have it, not for a minute!"

Something that had lain dormant in Robyn suddenly crystallised into firm resolve. She disliked the other girl and sometimes she was horribly jealous of her, but this was too much.

"*I* won't have it!"

Maria's mouth falling open in astonishment would have been amusing if Robyn had been in the mood to be amused. "I'm going to see her and bring her back right now," Robyn announced firmly. "There's a special way of treating staff in hotels in the islands and it isn't your way. Why don't you ask Mrs. Daley to show you how it's done? *She* never had any trouble with the native girls."

Before Maria could come back with a sarcastic rejoiner she turned away.

"But the craft shop, there'll be no one at the counter if you go!"

"That's your problem, you're in charge!" Robyn said, and

marched through the open porch and out into the sunshine outside.

As she hurried along the path she thought hotly of the injustice of Maria's treatment of Selani. Funny how she had endured so much in silence – Maria's maddening efficiency, the manner in which she contrived to make Robyn feel young and stupid and incompetent, especially when David were around; her habit of directing David's attention firmly in her own direction. Look at that night of the fire in the bures and the fainting attack by the pit of hot stones. On all of that Robyn had kept silent, but when it came to the Fijian girl, so pathetically anxious to please, so ill-matched for Maria's sophisticated dominance, Robyn had found herself hitting back without a second thought.

What matter that she had set herself a two-mile walk to the village during the hottest part of the day? Most of the route lay in the cool shade of thickly growing palm trees and clusters of tall bamboo and forest trees. Anyway, she thought angrily, she would gladly walk a distance twice as far to bring Selani back.

When she emerged from the shelter of the jungle growth, the sun beat down in a brilliant blue sky, striking her with fierce heat, but a short distance ahead of her were spreading trees and the scattered thatched huts of the native village.

She threaded her way between the lines of women, their beautiful tapa-cloth wares they had made from the crushed bark of the mulberry trees laid out on the grass. Soon she was standing at the entrance to one of the thatched bures and dazzled by the glare; it was a moment before she could focus her gaze on the Fijian girl who was bending over a stove at the end of the hut. The two small boys turned a shy gaze in her direction.

"Miss Carlisle!" A wide friendly grin lightened the island girl's face. "I thought I never see you no more." Salani rose from kneeling on the clean swept earth floor. "You like something to drink? A pineapple?"

"No, no, thank you, Selani. I just came to bring you back."

174

Tears welled up in the great dark eyes. "Can't come back, Miss Carlisle. That other one, she tell me –"

"It doesn't matter what Maria says. You're coming right back to the house with me! How can I manage without you to help me in the shop? You wouldn't want me to have to work there all day long and never have a single moment for my painting, would you?"

"But *she* say I can't come back. What if Miss Maria says 'No'?"

"Then I'll tell her that *she's* the one who will have to leave the Islander!" Could this be herself, so definite and determined, careless of consequences? I expect it's because I've finished with David and Maria. At last I'm myself. I don't have to worry about either of them ever again.

The wistful expression of the big-framed Fijian girl changed to a happy smile. "That all right then, if *you* say so, Miss Carlisle. But I have to wait until my sister comes back to tell her where I'm going."

"Of course." I can wait for ever. David won't be coming to the Islander now to take me to Suva. Probably he never really meant it when he said he would.

The younger child was whimpering softly, clinging to Selani's lonk skirts as she turned back to the stove. Afraid the child might venture too near the flames, Robyn picked him up in her arms. Tears still sparkled on the child's smooth brown cheeks and tenderly she wiped them away. "How about a smile? No? A kiss, then?" She pressed her cheek close to the child's face, conscious of a sense of comfort in the touch of the small soft body.

"May I come in?" David stood framed in the opening of the hut. It must be the shadows of the thatch that lent his face that odd expression as his eyes rested on her ... almost ... tenderness.

"It's Mr. Kinnear!" Selani, smiling broadly, was running eagerly forward.

"Hello, Selani. I heard you were over here, and Robyn too." In the dim interior he glanced from one to the other. "It's far too hot for walking, so I brought the car to take you both back. But I can see," he added pleasantly as the older boy set up a soft crying, "that you're a bit tied up at the moment."

Selani was glancing past him towards the opening and a moment later they were joined by a plump smiling Fijian woman. Smiling broadly, she said something in her own language.

"She tell you she pleased to see you," Selani translated. "She says you must have something to eat, drink –"

"Tell her thanks very much," David said smilingly, "but I've got to get these two back to the house. It's bad for business. Someone's got to be on duty at the craft shop, so shall we –"

The mother extended wide arms and Robyn transferred the small boy to the welcoming grasp. Then the three, waving farewells, moved out into the still tropical heat. David saw Robyn and the native girl seated in the car, then he thumbed the starter and soon they were turning into the rough road shaded by tall trees and thickly-growing bamboo.

Robyn swallowed. "Did you see Maria?"

He nodded, swerving to avoid an Indian youth riding a bicycle over the rough metal. "She told me there'd been a spot of bother and you'd taken off to fetch Selani back."

Maria would of course put it like that, giving him the impression of Robyn, foolish and unthinking as ever, rushing wildly away in the heat of midday instead of waiting to get someone to drive her to the village.

"She has no idea of how to treat the native girls, especially Selani," Robyn said hotly.

"Don't be too hard on her, Rob. She's new to the game here and she'll learn –"

Without warning the bitter anguish swept over her once again. Oh, she might have known he would take Maria's part! She steadied her trembling lips. "She hurt Selani's feelings terribly!"

"It won't happen again." He flung a glance towards the island girl in the back seat. "You don't mind giving it an-

176

other go, do you, Selani? You see Maria, she doesn't understand, but she's promised me that things will be different from now on. There won't be any more trouble of this sort."

Oh, she would promise anything for you! For one horrifying moment Robyn imagined she had spoken the words aloud.

When they reached the motel Maria smiled towards Robyn and spoke quietly and matter-of-factly to Selani, but Robyn had caught the secret glance that passed between Maria and David. It had all been arranged between them, just as they worked in together with everything. Apparently the island girl with her childlike capacity for happiness was prepared to forget the unpleasantness of the morning. It was only with Robyn that the incident still rankled. "I'd better get back to the shop," she said abruptly.

She had reached the door of the craft shop when David caught up with her. "On your way, Robyn! Selani's taking over this afternoon. I've just had a word with her and she's quite agreeable. Later on," he was regarding her with the smile that did things to her, made her immediately forget all her resolutions to put him out of her life, "we're taking off for Suva, remember?"

Her heart began its crazy thud-thud. So he had remembered! She turned a radiant face towards him. "You mean that party for Noeline and Johnny?"

"I mean," his tone was enigmatic, "the party for Noeline. You still want to go, do you?"

"Oh yes, yes, I do! It was just that I thought you had forgotten —" There, she had done it again, said the stupid words that were such a complete give-away as to her feelings. What was the use of ever trying to be offhand and careless? When she was with him things just didn't work out that way.

"I don't forget things like that, Rob." His tone lightened as he sent her his familiar bantering grin. "So why don't we take off right after dinner?"

"That would be nice." *Nice!* It would be heaven!

"It's a date, then."

Robyn still couldn't believe what was happening. David escorting her to a function, an invitation that had come from Noeline and Johnny. She couldn't fathom his object in going to this party and, Robyn-like, the words came thoughtlessly to her lips. "You know something, David?" She raised clear enquiring eyes. "I would have thought that this outing would have been just about the last place in the world you would want to take me to, or even to go yourself. I mean," suddenly she was confused, fumbling for words, "with Johnny there –"

For a moment he was silent, the dark eyes regarding her with a cryptic expression. "That's just why I'm taking you."

"But I don't get it –"

"You don't need to. Just come along with me, Rob, and we'll work it all out later."

She decided to take his advice. She was going with him to Suva. Just the two of them – no Maria. Tonight she would put everything from her mind except the joy of the moment. To him the ensuing evening would be merely an outing, but to her . . . A chance flung by fate to snatch a fleeting happiness, something to remember later when he had gone out of her life for ever.

Today her art work would be put aside in favour of more important matters. She washed her hair, thankful that the warm air would dry the long strands long before it was time for her to leave the motel. Later, meeting her reflection in the mirror, she was aware of a thrill of pleasure. Her hair, clean and shining with a patina of gold where the sun had touched it, fell around her shoulders. The cool white peasant blouse contrasted with the translucent tan of throat and arms. On an impulse she looped around her neck the long necklace of tiny shells that David had given her on their first visit to the native village. How long ago it all seemed now.

A knock and she opened the door to him. A dark man in a white turtleneck sweater, dark reefer jacket, grey slacks – and a look in his eyes that left no doubt whatever as to his approval of her appearance.

"Ready, Rob?"

⁵"Ready and waiting!" Funny how the moment she caught sight of him nothing registered but the subtle sense of excitement, the brittle transitory happiness. Together they moved along the passage and out into the warm star-pricked darkness of a Pacific night.

In the car a cool breeze from the ocean tossed Robyn's hair across her face. She pushed back the long strands and stole a glance towards David, his profile outlined in the dim glow of the dashboard. He intercepted her look.

"Happy?"

Happy! I'm always happy when I'm with you. "A bit." As always when she was with him, excitement stirred in her. They swept around the wide drive and turned into Queens Road, the main highway that followed the Coral Coast to Suva. Robyn put a hand to a switch, then immediately regretted the action as around them fell the haunting strains of "Isa Lei", the traditional Fijian song of farewell.

> "Isa Lei, the purple shadows fall
> Sad tomorrow will dawn upon my sorrow,
> Don't forget me
> When you are far away,
> Precious moments beside dear Suva Bay."

The refrain pierced her with a poignancy that brought a mist to her eyes.

As the native guitars faded into silence David flung her a teasing grin. "You like that song, don't you?"

"I guess," she said over the pain in her heart, "it's because it's more than just a song." The haunting melody threaded its way through the warm air, drifted on the breeze from ships and outriggers, echoed along the coast. "To me it's the essence of Fiji. It always will be."

"I know what you mean." He guided the vehicle around a sharp bend. "That song weaves its way through everything here, it's part of a way of life. Is it like you expected it to be, living out here in the islands, Rob?"

"Far more beautiful than I ever dreamed ... so colourful

179

the strange faces moving around her. Nothing else mattered but David and the soft intimacy of his gaze. Let Johnny keep his secret, whatever it might be. This was her night with the man she loved, a few precious hours filched from fate.

On only one occasion did David dance with anyone else, and that was when he partnered Noeline. As the other two moved towards the dance floor Robyn caught the other girl's excited tones. "I knew you'd come, that you wouldn't let me down!" The music of the Fijian group drowned out their voices as the other two moved away.

If only time didn't go by so swiftly. It seemed incredible that two hours had flown past already. All at once there was a roll of drums from the stage and the crowd gathered at the bar glanced around expectantly. In the sudden hush the dancers paused, looking towards the small family party grouped at the end of the big room. Of course, the special announcement Johnny had hinted at. How could she have forgotten? No wonder Noeline appeared so strung-up, two spots of vivid colour burning on the high cheekbones, her pale eyes alight with excitement. Robyn's glance slid towards Johnny. Even from a distance there was no mistaking his tense air of expectancy.

The older man had risen to his feet. "Folks, I've got a surprise for you, one of the reasons we invited you here tonight! It makes my wife and me very happy to welcome into our family a new son-in-law – Champagne, please –'" he gestured to a waiter and corks popped. "I give you Mark Sutherland, who I hope will make as good a husband as he does a business partner!" The dark thick-set young man standing a short distance away stepped forward and smilingly acknowledged the thunder of congratulations.

Robyn saw Johnny's face crumple as the varying emotions followed one another across his features – disbelief, shock, bewilderment. Her glance slid to Noeline and across the length of the big room the other girl sustained her gaze, a malicious smile of triumph curving the thin lips. So Noeline had won after all!

Robyn was only vaguely aware of the confusion of sounds around her, of David's hand, strong and comforting, on her arm. All her thoughts were for Johnny. His face deathly pale, he had flung around and was blindly pushing his way through the milling throng. "Johnny! Wait!" She tried to follow, but Fijian waiters carrying trays of drinks blocked her way and the surging crowd pushing forward to offer their congratulations to the newly-engaged couple hemmed her in. When at last she reached the door he had left the building. He couldn't have gone far. She glanced wildly around her, then became aware of David at her side.

"Let him go, Rob." His voice was very gentle. "He's got to work this out for himself."

She turned towards him grey eyes wide with fear. "But did you see how he looked? Like someone in a state of shock! He looked – desperate. In that mood he could do anything!" She scarcely knew what she was saying as the words tumbled wildly from her lips. "He's been counting on this for weeks. Don't you see, that's why he wanted us to come? Noeline must have led him along to believe all the time that the engagement announcement would be for her and him, and then he just couldn't believe it. Oh, David, did you *see* his face at that moment when he heard the announcement? I don't think he knows what he's doing just now, and if he's taken off in the car –" She stopped short as a vehicle screamed away from the line of cars and shot past them. For a second in the gleam of an overhead light, she caught a glimpse of Johnny's tense white face. Scarcely knowing what she did, Robyn tugged at David's arm. "Follow him, David! You've got to! In that mood he could do anything!"

With a swift glance at her distraught face, he turned. "Come on, then, Rob, let's go!"

Quickly they moved to the red car. Robyn threw herself inside and David slammed the doors, then they were taking off at speed up the main street. There was little traffic on the highway, but on the dark hill ahead a red light was fast disappearing into the distance.

183

David put his foot down on the accelerator and they flew up the hill.

"Do you think we can catch him?" Robyn's distraught gaze was fixed on the wavering needle of the speedometer. The other car was out of sight now around a bend on the winding road.

His eyes were on the highway. "I doubt it. With the hairpin bends at the top of the hill he's on a collision course. With luck we'll get there in time to pick up the pieces!"

He had put into words her own terrifying conclusions and as they sped up the bush-lined slope her anguished gaze was on the fragment of road illuminated in the twin arcs of the headlamps.

They were almost past the wreck when they glimpsed the shattered vehicle lying at the side of the road. Obviously travelling at speed, it had failed to negotiate the sharp bend. With a squeal of brakes David pulled up alongside and in a moment he was running towards the car lying on its side amongst the crushed palm trees. Robyn hurried after him. Just at first she didn't see the crumpled figure lying amongst the twisted trunks of coconut palms. Then David, kneeling beside the inert form, switched on his flashlight and she peered down over his shoulder. Johnny's eyes were closed, he lay so peacefully, almost as though he were asleep. Asleep! She caught her breath at the terrible fear that filled her.

"He's breathing all right." David's quiet tones were infinitely reassuring. "As far as I can see, there are no broken bones. Just concussion. Stay here with him, will you, Rob, while I go and call an ambulance."

It seemed an age, kneeling beside the still figure on the grass. There were times when she wondered if he were breathing, if David had merely been trying to allay her fears when he had spoken so reassuringly. At last car lights swept the ground as an ambulance braked to a stop nearby. Soon expert hands were lifting the unconscious man into the vehicle. David and Robyn followed in the car as the ambulance turned and sped back in the direction of the city.

Later, from the casualty ward of the hospital, a young doctor confirmed David's opinion as to Johnny's injuries. "He'll be fine in a day or two. Concussion, that's all, he was lucky! Just to be on the safe side, though, we'll keep him for a day or two to make certain there's no delayed concussion. After that you can come and collect him and take him home. Keep him quiet for a few days, that's all. He should come back to consciousness before long. Would you care to wait until then?"

"Oh, please!" Robyn raised a colourless face to David. "But there's no need for you to stay."

"Nevertheless, I'm staying." She thought, it's only because he's sorry for me. He's like that. But she couldn't help the warmth stealing around her heart.

It was only an hour later when Johnny's eyelids fluttered open. He tried to struggle up, then lay back on the pillows. Eyes wide with surprise, he stared at Robyn, seated by the bed. "Where . . . how . . . ?"

What a pity he has to know, she thought, but already she could see that remembrance was flooding back. "Last night I made a fool of myself."

"No, no, you didn't! It was Noeline who tried to do that."

"It's all coming back now." Dazedly he put a hand to his head. "I rushed outside and burned off in the car and then . . ." a look of bewilderment crossed the pale face. "The bend. I crashed, didn't I?"

"That's what happened," Robyn said gently. "The car looks as though it's a write-off, but as long as you're all right, that's all that matters."

"Who . . . found me, picked me up?"

"David and I. We followed you."

"I see. David. Why did it have to be —"

"You weren't capable of having much say in it, mate," David had come to stand by the bed. "Don't think of anything except getting on your feet again. The doctor says you'll be out of here in a day or so. Leave all the thinking until then, hmm? Meanwhile I'm taking Robyn home. She's been worrying herself sick about you and now that you're clear of the

185

danger zone she can relax and catch up with some sleep."

"Good idea." But she could see that Johnny's thoughts were elsewhere. "David, there's something . . ." She was aware of the struggle going on in his mind. Johnny always hated to admit defeat, to apologise. "I guess," he said gruffly, "things'll be a bit different from now on. At the Islander, I mean."

David shrugged broad shoulders. "It's up to you, mate. If you feel like taking over the running of the place, it's all yours. Go right ahead. Maria only came along to get the project off the ground. She's quite happy to move on somewhere else the moment you decide to take over the reins."

Robyn saw Johnny swallow, clear his throat. Johnny, who was never nervous, or if he were he never allowed it to show. "I wouldn't mind giving it a go." He moistened dry lips. "Last night's little show taught me a lesson, got it into my thick skull that there are some things that are a heck of a lot more important than money, debts, whatever. I mean, a guy can pay too high a price for a way out. Could be," he grinned his rakish, lopsided grin, "that things will work out after all . . ." His voice trailed away, his expression lighting up. "Especially," he added slowly, "if a guy had the right girl to help him along!"

As Robyn followed his gaze she saw a slim dark girl standing motionless in the opening, her gaze clinging to Johnny's face.

"*If* she's still interested," he added meaningfully.

"She is!" Pam, trim and attractive in her air hostess uniform, hurried to the bedside and clasped Johnny's outstretched hand. "I heard about the accident just after I got in on the flight this morning. One of the pilots had passed your car lying on the side of the road on his way to the airport. I came as soon as I could. How are you, Johnny?"

"Fine – now." His tone was threaded with happiness. "More than all right. Want me to prove it to you?"

His ardent glance brought the colour to her cheeks. Laughingly Pam turned away and seemed for the first time to be-

186

come aware of the other two. "David, and Robyn! But of course you were at the party last night too –"

"You know about that?" Johnny's voice held a plea for understanding.

"Couldn't help it. A hostess friend of mine happened to be there too and," Pam's voice softened, "she told me all about it!"

"Bet she didn't let you in on the main thing, though." All at once Johnny's voice was strong and decisive. "And that's the part I want you to know, Pam. I could have bought myself a load of trouble if Noeline hadn't had other ideas about the two of us teaming up together. Talk about a narrow escape! It's just coming to me how lucky I've been. A girl who'd do a thing like that to a guy ... but I guess it took something like that to open my eyes! You know something, Pam? With the right girl beside me I can tackle anything!"

To Robyn it appeared as though a terrific pressure had been lifted from his mind. It was wonderful to see the happiness in his face.

"Come along, Rob," David's voice was gentle, "I'll take you home." Swiftly they made their farewells and as they went along the quiet corridor she said ruefully, "I doubt if they even notice we've gone."

He threw her a grin. "That's love."

Love. She turned away, suddenly weary. It was almost over, the little time she'd had with him on the evening that was to be worth remembering, only it hadn't turned out like that. All she could remember now was Noeline's glance of triumph, Johnny's shocked expression. After the events of tonight she couldn't blame David were he to say "I told you so".

"Don't look so sad, Robyn!" He saw her seated in the car and they sped through the dark city with its lighted craft rocking at the harbour's edge. "He'll be as good as new tomorrow."

"Yes."

He threw his arm around her shoulders and she told herself that she was too discouraged to argue over it. But why not admit that in the comfort of his nearness her problems were magicked away and there was only the two of them, and the long drive back to the Coral Coast.

There was silence between them as they took the smooth road out of Suva and turned into the rough metal of the winding coast highway. Then Robyn, speaking her thoughts aloud, whispered, "You were right about Noeline. All the time it was revenge. She never cared a thing about Johnny, not really. She just couldn't forgive him for letting her down. He thought she'd forgotten, but a girl doesn't forget a thing like that, being thrown over just before a wedding. She must have gone to all the trouble of asking us to the party, making sure we'd be there when she made that surprise announcement. The bit about it I can't understand is –" She broke off.

"What can't you make out, Rob?" His voice was very gentle.

"Oh, just," he was in love with Maria so it didn't matter what she asked him, "why you said you'd come with me tonight."

"Can't you guess? I thought something like this might happen. I didn't want you to have to face it on your own."

"Nice of you." Oh, he could be kind, but what was kindness when you craved for love, all his thoughts, now, tomorrow, always. She summoned a wavering smile. "At least you didn't say 'I told you so'."

Lost in her thoughts, she scarcely realised they had left the main coast road and were turning down a rough track leading down to the beach. The sound of the surf was very loud as he ran the car down to the sand, drew to a stop and switched off the headlamps. Now there was only the moon-silvered sea and those incredible stars. Robyn felt her heart begin its heavy throb, throb. It was no use. She loved him so, she always would, even though she meant nothing to him.

Suddenly she was in his arms, very close, very happy.

"I love you, Robyn." He said it very quietly and for a moment she couldn't take it in for the wild sweet excitement that was surging through her. He said, very low, "I can't get you

188

out of my mind. Rob —" She didn't hear any more as his seeking lips found her own and the booming of the surf in her ears was majestic organ music drowning out everything else but ecstasy.

At last he released her gently. He traced the line of the small square jaw with his finger. "You do care?"

Flushed and tremulous, she met his steady gaze. "I always have, right from the beginning. I was so afraid you'd guess." As naturally as breathing, she snuggled into his arms. "You know, David, I always thought that you and Maria —"

"Maria?" There was no doubting the sincerity of his tones. "Believe me, Robyn my sweet, there was never anything like that between us! I was her husband's friend, that's all. She'd be the first to tell you the same."

Robyn was glad his kiss stopped her from having to make an answer. Privately she thought there were things that women knew about each other without having to spell them out. Things like Maria's coolness towards her that had nothing to do with matters at the Islander, the way she looked at David, the warmth in her tones when she spoke to him. Oh no, David my darling, it's not the way you think. With you, maybe, but not with Maria.

"It was just," she murmured against his bronzed cheek, "that you were always with her. That night of the fire in the bures, and when the firewalkers were performing —"

"Oh, now I get you! My darling, it wasn't like you thought. Maria wanted to keep the past out of it and I agreed to play along with that. There was a lot you didn't know about, sweet." His mouth brushed her lips. "You see, Rob, she had this thing about fire. You couldn't blame her when you knew the circumstances. I was there at the time it happened a year ago. Her husband Keith was a hotelier and he was killed by falling timbers when he was trying to rescue her from a blazing building. Ever wonder why Maria always wears long sleeves in her frocks, even in the heat of Fiji?"

"I have, sometimes."

"That's because she collected some shocking burns in the

189

tragedy. The scars are still there, though they'll fade away in time. She spent months in hospital afterwards. The shock of Keith's death, her own narrow escape, it all did something to her. Oh, I know on the surface she was cool and calm and frighteningly efficient, but underneath it all ... friends wrote me from Europe telling me that Maria was heading straight for a breakdown, her nerves were in a bad state still, and could I do something about it? That's when I arranged for her to come out here. I thought a new venture might take her mind off what had happened. The Islander, I figured, was just what she needed, a challenge, and a complete change of climate, surroundings, everything, might get the whole thing out of her system. Then what happens? The bures go up in flames the first night she arrives. I was afraid it would put her right back where she was six months earlier."

"So that was why you didn't want her to see the firewalkers that night?"

"That's why."

The thoughts rose to her lips. "And you went off with her—"

"It wasn't that I wanted to Rob. I never wanted to leave you, not for a moment. That's why I'm doing something about it." His usual lazy tones were warm and urgent. "Marry me, Rob, here in Fiji, just as soon as I can arrange it. You will?"

Her response to his caress was answer enough.

He carried her small brown hand to his lips. "You know what you've let yourself in for? Endless shifting around the islands—"

"I don't care!"

"No settled home—"

"I only want you."

"My darling ..."

Conscious of the strong pulse of life beating through her, Robyn knew that home to her would always be wherever they were together.

FREE

YOUR COPY OF OUR CATALOGUE
OF MILLS & BOON ROMANCES
NOW AVAILABLE

If you enjoyed this MILLS & BOON romance and would like a list of other MILLS & BOON romances available, you can receive a free catalogue by completing the coupon below and posting it off today. This opportunity to read more MILLS & BOON romances should not be missed. Your free catalogue will be posted off to you immediately.

To: MILLS & BOON READER SERVICE
P.O. BOX 236
14 SANDERSTEAD ROAD
SOUTH CROYDON CR2 0YG
SURREY, ENGLAND

Please send me my **free** copy of your latest catalogue of Mills & Boon romances

NAME .... MISS/MRS

ADDRESS ....

....

TOWN .... COUNTY/COUNTRY ...... MB 873

Mills & Boon's Paperbacks

SEPTEMBER

THE KISSES AND THE WINE BY VIOLET WINSPEAR

Lise wasn't keen on pretending to be the fiancée of an arrogant Spanish nobleman – but she had to agree for the time being . . .

CITADEL OF SWALLOWS BY GWEN WESTWOOD

Stacey was supposed to be marrying Colin, but found herself more and more disturbed by the imposing Greek Stavros Demetrios.

A TOUCH OF MAGIC BY ESSIE SUMMERS

Giles Logie had a reputation as a gay Lothario. So how had Lucinda managed to find herself posing as his fiancée?

ERRANT BRIDE BY ELIZABETH ASHTON

Antoine de Mericourt had married Sylvie to ensure that she concentrated on her career – but what about Sylvie's feelings?

CHASE A GREEN SHADOW BY ANNE MATHER

Tamsyn attracted Hywel Benedict as much as he attracted her – but marriage? No, he didn't seem to be interested . . .

THE GIRL FROM ROME BY NAN ASQUITH

Jane's fabulous summer in Rome was over – but would going to Corfu with Vance Morley help to solve her problems?

THE CRESCENT MOON BY ELIZABETH HUNTER

Stranded in Istanbul, Madeleine had no one to turn to but the lordly Maruk Bey. Could she trust him?

ISLANDS OF SUMMER BY ANNE WEALE

Working in Bermuda for the summer, Caroline would have been in Paradise – if it hadn't been for Ian Dryden!

BEWILDERED HEART BY KATHRYN BLAIR

Vernie wondered how she was going to cope with the heat of Nigeria She hadn't thought about the problem of Clin Peterson . . .

20p net each